WILLIAM

WILLIAM

A NOVEL

MASON COILE

G. P. PUTNAM'S SONS
New York

PUTNAM
— EST. 1838 —

G. P. Putnam's Sons
Publishers Since 1838
An imprint of Penguin Random House LLC
penguinrandomhouse.com

Library of Congress Cataloging-in-Publication Data

Names: Coile, Mason, author.
Title: William: a novel / Mason Coile.
Description: New York: G. P. Putnam's Sons, 2024.
Identifiers: LCCN 2023051938 (print) | LCCN 2023051939 (ebook) |
ISBN 9780593719602 (hardcover) | ISBN 9780593719626 (ebook)
Subjects: LCGFT: Science fiction. | Horror fiction. | Novels.
Classification: LCC PR9199.3.P96 W56 2024 (print) |
LCC PR9199.3.P96 (ebook) | DDC 813/.54—dc23/eng/20240220
LC record available at https://lccn.loc.gov/2023051938
LC ebook record available at https://lccn.loc.gov/2023051939

Export edition ISBN: 9780593854440

Printed in the United States of America
1st Printing

Book design by Laura K. Corless

To my family

1

Every morning felt like Henry's first. Perhaps it came from working with code so much, the detailed sequence of inconsequential numbers that resulted in something coming to life, something that had never existed before. Perhaps it was because his aversion to leaving the house had grown so severe that he'd long given up trying, so he was left with only one wonder within his reach. Lily. The woman sitting in the chair next to his bed, smiling in the lovely, vaguely haunted way he sometimes sees as a side effect of overwhelming love, and other times as merely pity.

"That was a bad one," she says.

"Was I snoring?"

"You were nightmaring. You woke up like I fired a gun next to your ear."

"Did you?"

Her glasses are round and too large for her face in a way Henry finds heartbreaking. She pushes them up hard against her brow. "What was the dream about?"

"It was the same one," he says. "More or less."

"Tell me."

"Why? Dreams are stupid. Don't we have other things—"

"Dreams tell us who we are," his wife says, and pulls the chair an inch closer, taps at her chin with doctorly interest. "Don't you think we could all use some help with that?"

He hears the "all" as meaning himself. *He* could use some help with knowing who he is. It's a very Lily thing to say: superficially supportive, curious, passively superior. His desire for her to stay here with him is so great he forgives her for making him feel like an anecdote, something she might later share with friends for their amusement. Or worse, their sympathy.

"It's our house. This house," Henry says. "I'm moving through the halls like I'm not in control of my limbs. Just drifting, you know?"

"Sure."

"And I'm going up the stairs to the second floor. That's when I start to get scared."

"Are you scared of—"

"Not it. Not exactly."

"So it's—"

"A sense. Like I know something bad is coming but I can't prevent it."

"And you can't wake up."

"I can't do *anything* except go where I have to go."

"The attic."

"The stairs to the attic, yeah. That's where I stop. Looking up at the door. Except it's different from the real door. This one is covered in chains and padlocks, top to bottom. Like whoever put them there didn't think there was enough of them so kept adding more and more."

There's no way to predict what will catch Lily's interest, and what will cause her to wander off and leave him to what she calls his "pet projects." Henry often feels like there's an undiscovered vein of conversation that might keep her with him longer, maybe even bring her back for good, if he could only stumble on the right topic or theme. He's made the mistake in the past of thinking she wants him to be more entertaining. But after trying to mimic the charm of the leading men in the movies she likes, he saw how she found him the least engaging when he was working the hardest at it. It makes him want to ask what she found most attractive about him before they were married—whatever quality he still possesses that he could try to magnify—but he worries she'll say she's forgotten.

"Then what?" she says.

"I hear a voice behind the door."

"Its voice."

"Yeah."

"But you couldn't hear what it was saying."

"When I've had the dream before I couldn't. But this time I could."

She sits straighter. "What was it?"

"It was quoting something. Lines from a book. A poem or novel. Maybe the Bible? Something it had memorized. It wasn't kidding around about it either."

"What do you mean?"

"The words weren't its own, but they were the truth of its being. Like another voice speaking through it."

"What did the voice say?"

"'I am the spirit of perpetual negation. For all things that exist deserve to perish.'"

"You *remembered* that?"

"I guess it was memorable."

"Shit." She shivers. A stagy gesture that builds into a genuine shudder. "*Perpetual negation.* Kinda grim, Henry."

"I wasn't appreciating the meaning of it as it happened. Only that, whatever it was, it meant it."

"At least that woke you up."

"No, that's not what did it."

"What did?"

The locks won't hold. That's what Henry recalls feeling, but he doesn't say it, because he doesn't want to frighten Lily. *Every chain and padlock in the world would make no difference.* Because what terrified him wasn't the thing on the other side of the wood, but the new thing that had joined it. A presence that will not be contained.

"A whisper," Henry says instead. "But when I got closer I heard it wasn't a whisper. It was a hand. Fingers stroking the inside of the door. And then—*boom!*—something smashed against it. Hard enough to split the wood. That's what woke me up."

Lily shudders again. "Well, you're here now."

"Where else would I be?"

"Good one," she says, and nods with a mixture of humor and sadness that he thinks of as her trademark, though sometimes wonders if he's reading it wrong. If maybe he always has. "Good one."

2

Things are bad between them, but not too bad. This is the estimation he's held to for so long it's become a truism, comforting as believing there's a heaven awaiting us after death. But sometimes, like now, he worries that his assessment of the bridgeable distance between himself and his wife is an error of judgment—the same made by millions of husbands right before the end. He doesn't normally wish he had friends, but when this thought comes to him, he does. It might be helpful to know a man of his age and experience who could tell him whether his troubles were benign or terminal.

But Lily's here now. There may be no magical words to keep her here, but showing his concern for her certainly couldn't hurt. As soon as he speaks, he sees how he may be wrong about this too.

"How are you feeling?"

"I'm pregnant, Henry, not ill."

"Of course. Of course not. I just know how it can make women uncomfortable sometimes. The process. Understandably."

"The process?" She laughs—briefly, resignedly—but not without some trace of warmth. *He's useless, but he's trying.* This is how he interprets it. Lately, it's been as good as it gets for him.

"When are we going to—"

"Don't."

"—talk about things?"

He raises himself up against the bed's headboard. His hand reaches out to her round stomach to feel the life inside her, but she pulls away. A flinch. Is that what he saw? Not a drawing back, the preference to not be touched, but a reflex of the body. It was as if she moved from him with revulsion, rather than anger or coldness or hurt.

"Not today," she says. "Soon."

"It's lonely waking up in this room alone."

"I know."

"How much longer do I—"

"Not *today*." She steps away so suddenly her glasses slide back down to the tip of her nose.

Henry was a fool when it came to marriage, and he worked to understand it with the flailing desperation of a drowning man fumbling with a life jacket. But he knew enough to know when to let a point go unpursued. Sometimes you had to wait for whatever bruise that ached between the two of you to darken first before fading, even if, looking back on it, you could never recall the blow that caused it in the first place.

Lily goes to the window at the far end of the room. "Curtain open," she says.

The heavy blackout curtains part on their own. The morning light first slashes, then expands through the space between the halves. It leaves Henry blinking where he still lies in the bed, in part from the brightness, in part to shield himself from the stark vacancy of the room. A single chair with wooden spindles along its back (their knobs poking and painful to sit against). A rug too small for the space, leaving the corners cold and exposed. The double bed of a size that can comfortably accommodate only one. The tidy vacancy of a spare bedroom.

"Window open," Lily says.

The heavy glass pane rises automatically. This time instead of light it's air that licks and curls against her skin. She breathes it in: the cool mineral scent of autumn that she thinks of as a cave turned inside out.

The sun pours down the street and splashes against the elms and cedar shake walls of her neighbors' houses, staining everything with orange and rust. It's the part of town where the rich once lived, the factory owners and physicians and distillers. After a few decades of neglect, a new set of professionals—start-up financiers and tech work-from-homers and consultants of niche expertise—had come to apply tasteful renovations and hang swinging love seats on the wraparound porches.

You could make fun of it as a nostalgic amusement park. Lily sometimes did, and in those precise terms. But it was also unquestionably lovely, the properties wide and deep, each façade an architectural defense of America, or the idea of it. It wasn't a gated community, but it made its values and exclusions clear nonetheless. The fantasy of the Upstate College Town, long thought to be extinct, but here returned to life on the handful of blocks on either side of them.

Even the morning's sounds were delightful. Birdsong and the babble of kids making their way to school on the sidewalk, the delivery drones dodging through the branches over their heads, buzzing like honeybees. Lily looks down at the parents herding their children or carrying them on their shoulders and guesses which of them she will seek out as friends once she joins their ranks.

It takes her a second to understand why the children themselves are dressed the way they are. Dwarfish superheroes and goalie-masked killers and green-faced, daycare-bound witches. The decorations on her neighbors' houses had been there the past couple weeks, but she'd grown used to them and forgotten why they were brought out in the first place. On almost every lawn there's a papier-mâché graveyard, every other tree home to a web of rope and a spider made of stuffed garbage bags. There are no such things on Lily and Henry's property. They have never decorated their house for this or any holiday.

"Halloween," she says.

"What?"

She speaks louder without turning around. "It's Halloween morning."

"Should we get candy?"

"Have we ever handed out candy?"

He thinks on this as if there's a riddle buried in it. "No," he says. "But we could start."

"We don't have a jack-o'-lantern by the door, no lights or decorations. Nobody is coming up our walk anyway."

"A trip to the store. That's all it would take."

Now she looks at him. A moment that stretches into a meaningful appreciation, her shoulders inching lower, yielding. "It's a nice idea. And it's sweet of you to suggest it. But I think we both know you're not going to the store, Henry. And even if you did—if you could—do you really see yourself opening the door to strangers?"

"You're right," he says, shaking his head. "I don't think I could manage it."

"Not without me having to call 911."

He snorts. It's his signal to her that concedes how their lives are shaped the way they are because of his deficiencies and his alone.

She crosses her arms over her chest and looks outside again, a pose he decides to read as contentment. He was wrong to pressure her to talk. Pregnancy brought on a chemical storm in the body, he'd read all about it. Which meant Lily was navigating herself through rolling waves invisible to him. It wasn't his place to demand her attention. And he had taken so much time for his work, for his creation, he's obliged to be patient now.

"There's lots in the fridge," he says. "I'll make us omelets."

She frowns. "You don't remember, do you?"

"Apparently not."

"We're having people over for brunch. Paige and Davis."

"I forgot. Your old co-workers."

"I thought it would be good for you to talk with people other than me for a change."

9

"It is," he says. "Good."

"I'm trying to help you."

"I know. But I have to do this on my own."

Once more she cocks her head at him in unexpected interest. "Do what?"

"Get rid of whatever's got me spooked up here." He taps the side of his skull. "And I think I can now."

"Why?"

"Because I know the cause of it. The more I've worked on my project, the worse the phobia got. So I'm going to pull back, and by the time the baby comes—"

"You don't need to—"

"—I'll be able to go outside."

She sucks her lips into her mouth and lets them pop wetly out. "What would you do if you could?"

"Push her in the stroller. Take her to the playground."

"Her?"

"I guess I've imagined it's a girl—not that it matters. I just don't want to be sick anymore. For her. Or him."

She sees his earnestness in this, and it softens her. The arms over her chest uncross, the hands rising—briefly reaching for him—before drifting back to her sides. "How are you going to do it?"

"Remember this moment. How I feel right now."

"An illness like yours—it's not just a matter of motivation, you know. It's not just *feelings*."

"You're right. It's a matter of will. Putting my mind to the things it should've been focused on for a long time."

"You *have* been focused," she offers. "You've been so involved in your project."

"Too involved. I'm sorry for that, too."

He has to do something. Right now. An opening has appeared, he's sure of it. This is the occasion for an emotional display, a spontaneous gift, a pleading. The kind of gesture he's always felt the most hopeless at. But the idea of Lily leaving with these questions clinging to them both has to be blunted in some way.

"I love you, Lily."

Her lips tighten into thin lines. It could be the beginning of a smile. The question of whether it's that or her readying to say an unkind thing is left unanswered when the little man in the top hat wheels into the room.

3

It takes a moment for Lily to assemble the details of what she's looking at.

A doll wearing a star-covered cloak with a black top hat roughly stitched to its head, riding a bicycle. A plastic circle of a face rouged with cherry cheeks and a wide, oval mouth that suggests some unwholesome exertion. It's only a foot high and proceeds with the certainty of a puppy tripping on its own ears, but its movements are less comical than unsettling. Each part is store-bought but augmented by hand: the motorized knees, the ill-fitting magician's outfit. A customized mutant.

Lily takes an involuntary step back, but it decides on her as its target. Squeaking and wobbling forward, its knees jutting out from under its cloak and disappearing again with each thrust. The top hat is loosely attached to its scalp so that it slides forward and back, over and over. Now it hangs over its forehead, hiding its face, leaving its chin its only visible feature. The pubic fuzz of a black goatee.

"Well," she says. "This is new."

"That's weird. I thought I turned it off before I went to bed."

"What *is* it?"

"A little magician. Riding a bicycle."

"Right, I can see that. I guess I'm asking why you'd make it?"

"It's a balance study. To see if I could get it to pedal without falling. A preliminary test for William when I build him out and give him ambulatory—"

"Can you turn it off?"

"It's probably only got an hour or so left on its battery anyway, so—"

"Can you? Please? I don't like it."

She's watching the mini magician squeak around her feet in a circle, its black top hat resuming its bobbing up and down in a way Henry assumed would be cute but sees now is perverse.

Henry gets out of bed, bends down on one knee, the sides of his hands on the floor in an open V, ready to corral the toy. But when its pedaling knees and lewdly pumping hat come around the corner of Lily's shoes and start toward Henry, the magician does something unexpected. It pivots the handlebars to the right, almost toppling but not quite, veering hard away from him.

"It's trying to get away," Lily says, half-alarmed, half-impressed.

"It's supposed to come to me. I guess it thinks my hands are a wall or some other object to avoid."

"Huh. So can you control it? Or are we just living with it rolling around the house?"

"Its direction command is connected through the Wi-Fi. I'd have to log in to pull it up."

"Okay. Are you going to *get* it, then?"

"It's not going anywhere."

"Well, it *is*, because it's out in the hall now."

She's right. He can hear it squeaking over the floorboards. Another surprise. It made it out the door much faster than it managed before, during his tests.

Henry stalks out of the bedroom and into the hall, telling himself to move decisively but without excessive haste. A man in control. A man headed off to reassert normalcy in his home. A man.

The little magician is rolling toward the bottom of the attic stairs. It's getting better at riding the bicycle even as Henry watches it. The possibility occurs to him that the toy was previously only pretending to wobble. An act, even as he knows there's no way for it to formulate that kind of strategy.

He catches up to the little magician just as it turns to avoid hitting the bottom step of the stairs. Henry looks up at the door at the top, the door from his nightmare. This one secured by a single padlock instead of a dozen. No chains. He wishes, ridiculously, that there were.

"Abracadabra!" he announces, sweeping the bicycle and its rider off the floor, its cloak flapping.

He pops up the hinged top hat and puts his thumb down on the power button he'd located in the crown of its skull. The battery must have expired at about the same time, because Henry could swear that the little magician stopped pedaling and went still a half second before the button was pressed.

He looks back down the hall to find Lily standing outside the spare bedroom. She saw it too. The gap between the magician playing dead and Henry turning off its power.

"Got the little fucker," he says.

Lily turns and starts down the stairs, so that he can't see whether she is fighting tears or some other inclination.

4

The house is one of the enormous Victorians up the slope from downtown. It presents as old, is full of old things, and was owned by a series of old people over the years, each of whom left by way of the undertaker's box. But if you look closely the house reveals all the ways it's different.

To turn on the lights, to make the water hotter, to open, close, and lock the doors—everything is done by the command of either Henry's or Lily's voice. The whole place is wired, but subtly so. Aside from discreet keypads located in the walls here and there, it appears traditional: original brick fireplaces on the main floor and guest bedroom, pine cabinets in the kitchen, furnishings bordering on old-fashioned. Yet the house is cybernated to a degree far beyond the capacity of any store-bought smart device or talking appliance.

And Henry did all of it himself.

After what he calls his "symptom onset," he converted the third-floor attic into a lab and asked Lily to have the security system and other hardware pieces shipped to the house so he could personally modify each one before installing them. The asking-Lily part is an unspoken agreement between them: she manages the expenses. Virtually all the money is hers, anyway, after the stock sale of the software company she founded, so it makes sense. And by Henry's own admission, he's a dunce at negotiating with salespeople or tracking the costs of things, the "real-world stuff" his wife has always been better at.

They're both engineers. He's robotics, she's computers, though "there's tons of overlap," as he likes to remind her, always on the lookout for common ground. They met in postgrad, where they were stars in their respective fields before sharing a lab where their expertise comingled on joint projects. They fell in love with the work. They fell in love. He's far more confident in saying precisely when the former happened than the latter.

At some point along the way they agreed to their casting: he's the socially awkward nerd with untreated neuroses, she's the business savant sitting on millions but restless for more. More money, it's assumed, though the possibility that it may be something else is one of the aspects that goes unsaid.

Henry frequently reviews this history of his life with Lily—as he does now—in the hope that it will remind him of the enduring substance at the foundation of their union. After all, he was the one she chose, and not one of the other candidates who mumbled and struggled to make eye contact around her during those years. But the recollection only highlights all the alternative decisions she could have easily made.

What's important is to affirm what makes him special. Right now that's his creation. The thing on the other side of the attic door.

He starts up the stairs without intending to, as if summoned. Each step a heavy confirmation of his reluctance.

"Unlock lab door," he says.

The chunky clack of the bolt retreating from the slot. The padlock next. Henry pulls a key from his pocket. He takes a breath and hears it whistle through his tightened throat.

"Open lab door."

5

The robotics lab takes up the entire attic of the house. A chaos of desks covered with hard drives and monitors, one large table piled with rubber masks and plastic body parts. A bare foot atop a technical manual as if it had just stomped its cover shut. An arm hanging over the table's edge, reaching for a bruised apple on the floor. The overhead LEDs drop white cones of light, leaving the rest of the room in shadow.

Henry steps into the room and tries to appear relaxed, even though his arms tense up involuntarily, as if to block a charging attack.

"Here I am."

The voice is deep, almost tranquilized. The hint of a slur, as if coming from an end-of-the-night drunk bringing the last shot to his lips. But there is no weakness in it. A voice that suggests a body of experience best left unexplored.

"I don't see you," Henry says, and his own voice is like an empty soup can dropped in the street.

"Over here."

It takes a second for Henry to find his creation sitting on a stool in the corner.

The robot holds a pocket-sized transistor radio to its ear, listening to what sounds like Broadway show tunes. From the beginning, it has listened to the world this way, switching radio stations seemingly at random. Kiddie pop to country, shock jock to NPR. It occurs to Henry that the radio is the only gift it has ever received without asking.

> *Whether I find a place in this world or never belong*
> *I gotta be me, I've gotta be me*

The robot clicks the radio off and sets it on the nearest desk. Its movements are slower than a human's, premeditated, as if it were moving chess pieces according to a pattern it had foreseen in its mind.

"Thank you for the books," it says.

The robot extends a hand, wavering and lethargic as a snake's head, and picks up a paperback from the top of a stack. A dozen at least. The pages puffy from moisture, the covers curled brown at the corners.

"This was my favorite," it says. "*Faust*."

"You read all of them?"

"Some twice. The good parts, anyway."

"I only gave those books to you yesterday."

"It was a long night." It strokes the cover of the paperback in its hand. "Have you read it?"

"No."

"I think you'd find it resonant."

"Oh?"

"An ambitious man strikes a bargain with a demon he believes he can control—a contract signed in blood that forever joins the two—"

"I don't believe in the supernatural."

"But you're my creator. And what's natural about me?"

The robot—Henry has named it William—leans forward an inch and is partially revealed under the nearest spotlight.

William is dressed in what it calls its "Sunday best" even though it's the same outfit it wears every day. An itchy tweed suit. A tie hung loose, its knot fat as a fist. The shirt too small at the neck but it's buttoned to the top nonetheless, so that the collar squeezes its throat like a noose. The thick material, the tight shirt—to look at it makes Henry feel feverish even though the attic is air-conditioned cool.

Because Henry has built William on his own, and because his focus has been on the machine's consciousness and not its body, the robot is disturbing to look at. Sometimes, as now, Henry finds it a little frightening. There's something unnatural—something *off*—about every aspect of its appearance. The face most of all. Fake skin the texture of balloon rubber covers its steel skull. Bulging eyes, round as marbles. Ears the size of ashtrays, the color of curdled milk. All of this prevents it from ever being mistaken for human no matter the distance, no matter how it clings to the shadows.

Its body is no better. In fact, it's only half a body: torso, arms, head. Pants belted tight and high on its chest, the legs empty, hanging over the side of the stool like a pair of windless flags.

"You seem excited this morning," William says. "Did your wife finally pull back the bedsheets and let you in?"

Henry knows it's best not to respond to the robot's provocations. It only tilts the balance of their exchanges in William's favor, as it is far more adept at finding what makes Henry angry than the other way around. In fact, Henry isn't sure William is capable of anger. A buried, shapeless hate, perhaps. Henry has caught glimpses of that. But not the anger he feels rising now.

"I would ask you to mind your own business," Henry says.

"But I *have* no business. I have no legs to take me to a place where I might *find* my business. And as you won't allow me out of this room, my business is limited to you."

"I'm sorry I'm not more interesting company."

"Oh, you're interesting enough," William says, every word clotted with falsehood.

The robot tosses the paperback onto the table, where it spins in place before coming to rest with its spine facing Henry. With the same hand it struggles to gain a hold on the table's edge, its narrow, pencil-long fingers slipping off the varnished wood. Once the fingertips stay in place for more than a second, it pulls.

Henry expects the robot to topple to the floor but instead the stool slides forward with a high, mousy squeak. With its free hand William fumbles at the edge of a different table and does it again. A pull, a squeak, pull, squeak. In the poor light it appears to advance by an impossible combination of tickling and levitation.

"You put wheels on your chair," Henry says.

"I hope you don't mind. You leave so many useful things lying around."

"Mind? I'm impressed."

"A low threshold. I can't do the foxtrot yet but it's better than nothing."

Henry doesn't like the way it can move now. It's not only the fact that it can, but the way it does. The pale hands fondling the table edges. The casters shrieking over the floor. The look of triumph the robot attempts to shape with its palsied face.

"I'm curious," Henry says. "Where do you think those wheels are going to take you?"

"I don't know. I suppose the four corners of my cell."

"This isn't a prison."

"You know that it is. We're both inmates, after all."

"That's not—"

"Ever wonder why you can't walk away from this place?"

Henry is aware he shouldn't answer but has no alternative to not answering. Leaving the robot with the last word? Going over and kicking the stool out from under it? Everything he might do is worse than engaging William on its own terms.

"It's an anxiety disorder," Henry says. "I've already told you."

"You've told me a lot of things."

"I wish I hadn't."

"You have to trust somebody, don't you? Not sure about your wife, to be honest." William cocks its head as if the thought is just occurring to it. "How are you sure she isn't the cause of your disorder?"

"Because I love her."

The robot laughs at this. A thick gurgling in its throat that's close to choking.

"You're lonely for 'love,' stuck in here for 'love.'"

"You don't know anything about it. You couldn't."

"I know you need to get out. You need to feel all there is of the world."

"I don't need the world. I just need her." Henry realizes he shouldn't have said this. None of it, but this last sentiment most of all. It's too revealing, too honest, too weak. But then he says something even more revealingly honest and weak. "My family."

"Then your problem isn't anxiety. It's lack of appetite."

From two floors below they hear the doorbell ring. It's such an unfamiliar sound that Henry startles. William appears to stiffen too, though not with surprise. It's the keen attention of an animal smelling far-off prey.

"Who's that?" the robot says.

"We're having guests."

William curls its tongue against the inside of its upper teeth. One of its tics that Henry has come to see as distinctly reptilian.

"You never have guests," William says.

"We do today." Henry backs away but doesn't want to let the robot out of his sight, so he lingers at the lab's threshold. "I have to go."

"Before you do, do me the favor of telling me who's at the door."

"Friends."

"Not yours, surely."

"Co-workers of Lily's. Former co-workers."

"Employees," William clarifies. "Lily owned the company."

"Did I tell you that?"

Henry has no memory of this. It's the sort of thing he'd be careful not to share with William, but he supposes it's possible, in some underslept moment, that he had.

"You should go," William says, ignoring the question. "Your wife's friends will be anxious to meet the mystery husband."

It's only on the way down the stairs that Henry realizes he hadn't told William he'd never met Lily's friends before.

6

Henry pauses five steps from the bottom of the main staircase, out of view of the people standing in the living room off to the right but close enough to hear them.

Along with Lily there's a man and a woman. The woman's voice is at once low and grating. It makes Henry think of the growl of a snowplow and the intermittent shrieking of the blade connecting with pavement. The man sounds handsome. Henry can't explain how or why, but it's unmistakable. As if he's sure of who he is in a way Henry never sounds, even to his own ears. Henry tries to carve the man's voice into one that would belong to someone smarmy or squat or unlikable but can't quite make it work.

"I wasn't expecting everything to be so damn old," the woman says.

"Not old," the man says. "Antique."

"You wanna tell me the difference?"

"I will," Lily says. "A thousand percent markup."

The three of them laugh like actors in a play. That's how it sounds to Henry anyway. A classy, Broadway production cast with Ivy Leaguers playing Ivy Leaguers, laughing along with the audience at the dumb world outside the theater walls.

"Is the man of the house coming down to join us?" the woman says, her lips smacking around "man."

"Any minute," Lily says. "Henry likes to check in on his lab first thing."

"What's he working on up there?" the man says.

"I'm not entirely sure," Lily says. "He's very private about it. Calls it a 'work in progress.'"

"Probably just filling up a hard drive with porn," the woman says, and congratulates herself with a single honk of laughter.

"This is why you don't get invited places, Paige," the man says.

"Oh, c'mon, I'm fun at parties," she says. "Ask anyone who's thrown me out of one."

Henry listens to them step out of the living room, and he leans against the wall to prevent being seen. They clip farther down the main-floor hallway into the dining room, where they continue to talk but now their words are indistinct, a murmuring of collegiality and ease he finds alienating.

He has delayed and spied and talked himself through the various approaches he should take, and now there's no time left. He goes the rest of the way downstairs.

With his first step he thinks he hears a thump from the attic. Probably the robot heaving itself around the lab on its homemade wheelchair, though it seems louder and more abrupt than that. A book dropped from a standing height. A fist punched into a wall.

* * *

Henry makes his way to the dining room so quietly—or their continued talking is so loud—that Lily and her guests don't notice him standing in the alcove. He watches as, one by one, they feel his presence there. The woman who must be Paige notices first, then the man, then Lily. Watching him now, but after all their chatter, saying nothing.

"The table looks beautiful," Henry says.

Lily goes to him, takes his arm in a demonstration of affection but, in its firmness, feeling more nurselike in support.

"Henry, these are my colleagues," she says. "From Interron. You remember me talking about them all the time. Paige. And Davis."

Henry is ready to say *Hello, welcome, thank you for coming*, but holds back. *You remember me talking about them all the time.* Lily had mentioned these two, yes, but not often. He supposes this is polite exaggeration on her part. Elevating her guests to special status. But it also makes him wonder whether he's the one being misled. Lily speaking of Paige and Davis only rarely had him believing they were nice enough but ultimately unimportant.

The seconds it takes for Henry to think this allow Davis to come to him and pump his hand in a firm shake. Henry was right about the man's voice. He's good-looking. The slices of dimple alongside his mouth, the square shoulders of the once-serious athlete. His warmth is effortless and, as far as Henry can guess, genuine.

"We've heard so much about you," Davis says. "It's kind of un-believable we're actually here, meeting you in the flesh."

"What did you hear?"

Davis wasn't expecting this. He looks to Lily as if a referee who could wave off the play, but she remains still.

"That there's nobody like you," Davis says. "That's what Lily was always saying."

"An agoraphobe with a serious antisocial streak who's working alone in his home on a project he won't share with anyone." Henry laughs. A bitter, self-deprecating bark. "Yup. I'm one of a kind."

Henry shifts his attention to Paige, who is openly staring at him. He notes the wasted efforts that have gone into her appear-ance. The naturally curly hair half straightened into crispy waves. The expensive jacket with sleeves that come down to her knuck-les. The eyebrows trimmed down to a pair of graphite lines drawn straight as a ruler.

"You didn't tell me how gorgeous he is," Paige says.

Henry is put off by this frank assessment, glances at Lily, who again offers no help.

"I'm standing right here," he says.

"Okay," Paige says. "How gorgeous *you* are."

"Paige can sometimes speak before she thinks," Lily says.

"Doesn't make it any less true." Paige passes her eyes over Henry in a way that makes him think of a tongue.

"Your sleeves are too long," Henry says.

He's only trying the same thing—the unguarded assessment—back at her. There is no hostility in it. It's a spontaneous social ex-periment. If this woman can say anything in the name of truthful evaluation, can he do the same? Judging by Lily's expression—not to mention Paige's—the answer is no.

"I'm *sorry*?" Paige says, looking down at the ends of her jacket's sleeves as if at the blameless faces of her own children.

"Never mind," Henry says. "Just distracted for a second."

Paige continues to draw her eyes over him, but now it's not a tongue he thinks of but a razor blade.

"Maybe we should eat?"

This is Davis. He's trying to help. Help Henry, specifically. There's even a passing look he offers that seems to say *Don't worry, she bugs the shit out of me sometimes too*. And while Henry appreciates it—he can't stop himself from appreciating it, as he so often wishes for similar lifelines from Lily—he also resents it. This is his house. He doesn't need this almost-stranger to rescue him.

"I think that's a good idea," Lily says, and releases Henry's arm.

7

There's way too much food. Did Lily expect more guests that couldn't make it at the last minute? Smoked salmon, croissants, a charcuterie platter, chopped salads, multicolored spreads and dips. All of it catered. Lily likes to say she "microwaves, but doesn't cook." And Henry is no foodie.

The four of them circle the long dining table, piling their plates with an enthusiasm meant to put the previous moment's awkwardness behind them. Henry hears their banter but barely registers what they're saying about the food as he's doing his best to keep what he hopes is an amused ease set over his cheeks and brow. He's aware of how working to appear relaxed makes the performance all the less convincing. He's never been good at this version of "fun," and he's gotten worse at it over the last couple of years. Ever since the symptom onset. His phobia. Anxiety. Illness. Whatever you choose to call being unable to leave your own home without the certainty that, by taking a single step, you're going to die.

"Thanks for having us, Henry," Paige says, her plate a sculpture of excess. "After Lily sold the company and made her millions, we figured she'd be too good to hang out with schmucks like us again."

Henry looks to his wife. "She's loyal that way."

He meant it literally, but all of them immediately hear its acidic alternative. *Oh yeah. She's loyal to schmucks, alright. Including me.* It's self-pitying and bitchy where he didn't intend it to be. To avoid their eyes he adds a second croissant to his plate that he has no plans to eat.

"I hear you've got a number of projects on the go," Davis says, again coming to Henry's aid.

"Probably too many for my own good."

"Robotics, right? Your training?"

"That was then. Now? I make toys. I'm a regular Geppetto."

"That's not true," Lily says. "There's your main project."

"Nobody has seen *that* yet. For good reason."

"What's the good reason?" Paige says.

"It's not ready."

Henry shrugs. The idea of speaking about William with this woman makes an itch roll down his skin from the crown of his head.

"And you do your work all on your own?" Davis says, ignoring Paige on Henry's behalf.

"Lily keeps me stocked in the gear I need. I'm a one-man start-up."

"Listen," Paige says. "If Lily is backing you, she must see a way to monetize your Pinocchios."

"I'm her husband," Henry says. "She has no choice but to back me."

Lily shrugs at this—*Well, that's not exactly true*—and pretends to be reading something on the tiny square of blue on the inside of the right lens of her glasses. It's a connection to her computer that she can check with a tap at one of the frame's arms, then make it disappear again with a long blink. There were occasions Henry thought she was gazing at him, trying to dig deep to some essential part of him, only to realize she was remotely scrolling through her email.

"I'm curious," Paige says to him. "Do you work out?"

"Exercise?"

"Yeah. Like, a routine? It's just that Lily tells me you're quite the homebody, so I figured you had some way of, you know, letting off steam—"

"Excuse me," Henry says.

"Where are you going?" Lily says.

"The bathroom. Upstairs."

"Okay," she says doubtfully.

He makes his way out of the dining room with their judgment prickling his back like acupuncture needles.

* * *

Henry doesn't have to use the bathroom. The morning requires a fresh approach, and he needs to decide how to go about it.

What's important isn't matching Davis's self-certainty or pretending to find Paige refreshing and edgy. It's Lily. Their baby. Their *home*. Showing their guests how, despite the idiosyncrasies of their domestic life, he and his wife are committed to each other. They've come through challenges. He has a debilitating psychological disorder he's making headway on. They've made their partnership work. They're going to have a baby and, boy or girl, it will be safe and loved.

It only leads to a new problem. Or a different view of the same one.

How do you prove that you're normal and worthy?

But that's not the only thing troubling him. There's Davis too.

The comfort he clearly feels in being here is both a result of his natural composure and another unacknowledged advantage. Information he possesses that Henry doesn't. A connection to Lily that is a different shape from merely "co-workers." Maybe Paige knows it too. This is why she feels free to tease Henry, assess him so baldly.

Henry lets his mind tumble down this paranoid path as he walks past the second-floor bathroom and stops at the stairs up to the attic. No sounds from the other side of the lab door. No punches or dropped books. No caster wheels rolling and squeaking. No recitation of apocalyptic verse.

But he does hear voices.

He can't make out the words. Or even if they are words. Two voices, though. There's an almost singsong quality to the exchange to suggest they could be hummed lyrics, or a chant. One is William. The other voice is at an even lower register, a bass note that Henry feels in his chest more than he hears in his head.

As soon as he's certain of what he's hearing, the voices stop.

Henry listens, and his listening only deepens the quiet from the other side of the attic door. He feels sure this is because whatever is there listens and reaches for him too.

8

Henry retreats down the hall. He can't rejoin the others yet, not until he's sure he's calmed the nerves that the attic voices have electrified in him. It's why he lingers outside the one room in the house he goes to when he needs reassurance.

"Nursery door open."

He slips in sideways, keeping his eyes on the attic stairs as if expecting some creature to come scuttling down. He only loses sight of the stairs when the nursery wall blocks it from view.

The room has been lovingly assembled: an electric train set in an oval on the floor, a wooden crib with a doll on its back and stuffed animals standing guard around it, a baby penguin mobile hanging over them all. On the ceiling a constellation of glow-in-the-dark stars and full moon.

He chose everything himself. Lily was consulted, of course,

and he tried to solicit her opinion on each item, but she was content to let the nursery be another one of his obsessions.

"The baby will grow out of all this before you know it," she said once when he pulled her in to show how everything had come together.

"It's not for the baby. Not really," Henry said. "It's for us. For you."

She pursed her lips to communicate her gratitude, though it left him feeling like he'd done too much. Or not enough. But what hurt him was the coldness she showed toward the doll.

It was chosen for its similarities in appearance to Lily herself. The narrow, dark brown eyes. The pixie nose. The flower bud ears.

He picks up the doll and holds it as he guesses to be the right way to hold a real baby, notched into the cradle of his arm. The eyelids are still closed. They're supposed to open with a change in the angle, the tilt of the head. Henry shakes the doll slightly. One eye pops open. He's doing it wrong, holding it wrong. In trying to show his love he's hurt the baby without meaning to.

He lays the doll back in the crib, carefully placing its head on the mattress. The eyelid slides shut.

Enough time has passed that they'll be wondering what's taking him so long. The last thing he needs is Lily—or worse, Paige—coming up to find him here, eyes jellied with tears.

Yet he lingers a moment longer. Picks out the handheld baby monitor from the crib. Flicks it on.

The screen reveals what the camera affixed to the corner of the ceiling sees: the crib in clear, black-and-white night vision. And Henry standing there. Still as a mannequin.

He waves at the camera to confirm that he's able to, proof he's alive, and there's a fraction of time—a millisecond lapse between his movement and the image on the monitor held in his palm—when he worries nothing will happen and he will remain frozen as the doll he'd just been holding.

* * *

When Henry returns to the dining room there's only Paige sitting at the table, spreading cream cheese on a bagel.

"I was going to send out a search party," she says. "Meaning me."

"Where's Lily?"

"Cleaning up. Come over here and sit. You haven't eaten a thing. And this smoked Spanish ham is *insane*—"

"And Davis?"

"He's helping Lily in the kitchen."

"I should give them a hand."

"What? Why? They've got it covered. And I've got so many *questions* for you."

"I'm sure. Just give me a second."

"I'd give you anything, sweetheart."

Did she just say that? He's already turning the corner to the hallway and moving toward the kitchen. *Sweetheart?*

These thoughts are overtaken by a new, more pointed one. *Why are you sneaking up on them?* Without thinking about it Henry crosses the last few feet to the kitchen almost on tiptoes. He slows down just before he gets to the doorframe.

Davis is finishing what sounds like a plea, or rebuttal. His voice started out as a whisper moments earlier but is now slightly raised in exasperation.

"—not now, then when?"

"When I'm ready."

Davis takes a deliberately calming intake of air that doesn't work. "We need to tell him."

"Don't."

Henry slides forward and looks around the corner in time to see Davis put his arm around Lily, his hand at the small of her back. An intimate contact she stiffens against at first, the tea towel she'd been using to dry a china platter swinging against her side. Henry waits for her to pull away or slap him or call out in protest. But a second later all she does is lean into the man's touch.

"I don't feel right being in this house," he says. "It's not—"

"Hold on—"

"—it's not right."

"I get to decide that."

"I'm not sure that's true. Not anymore. You have to tell—"

Henry forces himself to step into the room. He tries to do it at the same speed he would have been moving if he'd walked straight from the dining room without pausing. Whatever it was that he saw before has to stop. He doesn't want to think about why.

"Hey," he says. "I have an idea."

They look at him. Davis's hand slowly drifts away from Lily's back as if returning to his side after scratching his nose.

"Okay," Lily says.

"Let me show you."

"Show us what?"

"Him," he says. "William."

Lily stands still. For a moment Henry wonders if she's heard him, or if the baby has wriggled inside her and drawn her thoughts away, or if she's uncomfortable with the way he's said "him" in reference to something that, until now, was an "it" between them.

"Now?" Lily says.

"If you have time. If you're interested."

"It's just—you've been so *private* about this."

"You deserve to see what's stolen my attention for so long."

Lily and Davis share a glance. Or something smaller than that. A simultaneous twitch.

"So let's see it," Lily says, and tosses the wet tea towel into the sink. "There's no one like you in the world, Henry."

He tries to cool the blushing heat in his cheeks but there's no stopping it, so he lets it set fire to his heart.

"Follow me," Henry says.

9

The four of them troop up to the second floor with the heaving steps and hoarse breaths of mountaineers. Each a little drunk on a cocktail of hesitance and anticipation.

As they march down the hall a dog emerges from Lily's bedroom.

The size of a Labrador. Or even bigger. Tail wagging. A tennis ball in its mouth. It trots on legs so stiff it hops from side to side in order to move forward. When it comes to Henry's feet it stops, looks up.

All of them see now that it's not a regular dog. Its fur is patchy, glued on. The ears rotate like radar dishes. The eyes make a sound—*whirr-whirr*—as their lenses adjust into focus. The dog utters a low woof, dry as whooping cough.

"Not now," Henry says. "We'll play later."

The tail droops in disappointment.

"You made this?" Paige says, coming to stand just behind Henry as if the dog might leap at her throat.

"Yes."

"Does it have a name?"

"I call it Dog."

"Wow. That must have taken you all day to come up with."

"Henry is very talented," Lily says. "He makes the most wonderful devices."

"It's amazing," Davis says.

"It's hideous," Paige says.

"There's more to things than how they look," Henry says, stepping away from Paige and leaving her unprotected.

Henry continues up to the door at the top of the attic stairs telling himself he's not worried, not afraid, but the truth is he has always been a little worried, a little afraid. He feels these things every morning as he makes his way to his workspace. Only more so today after last night's dream. The certainty that there is something new, something worse behind the door.

I just hope—

He can't decide between the different ways he might complete his thought.

I just hope he's in a good mood.

I just hope he can't see how nervous I am.

I just hope he doesn't—

He places his hand on the doorknob.

"Unlock lab door," Henry says, and turns to the others behind him. "Give me a minute with him first."

* * *

The robot has his back to Henry in the far corner of the lab. He's doing something with his hair. Stroking his hands over his head, using his fingers as the teeth of a comb. Henry sees that William does this while looking at himself on a laptop screen, the built-in camera returning a bright image of his drooping, carelessly assembled face.

"I've brought you some visitors."

William goes still. He was so engrossed in his self-examination he hadn't heard Henry come in, or had pretended not to. The robot's hands close the laptop. He straightens his shoulders before turning to face Henry.

"Who?"

"Lily," Henry says. "And her guests."

"Why haven't you shown me to anyone before now?"

"You weren't ready."

"But that's not the whole truth, is it?"

William pulls his way between the tables on the wheeled stool. He's gotten better at it even since Henry's earlier visit. Now the grabbing and yanking of his overlong arms give the unnerving impression of an orangutan, a hidden capacity for swinging and flying.

"You're not sure if I'm something to be proud of or ashamed of," the robot says. "Good. Or bad. But it shouldn't trouble you either way."

"Thanks for the—"

"All those moral evaluations—they're handcuffs. You could be free of them like that"—he clicks his fingers—"if you chose to be, brother."

"Don't call me that."

It comes out sharper than Henry intended. The robot knows he hates being called this. It's why he so frequently uses the term.

Henry finds the calm line in his voice again before speaking. "I just need you to be at your best."

"Best? I can't even walk." William reaches down and shakes one of his empty pant legs. "And my face. Couldn't we wait until you work up something a little less horrific?"

"Your vanity surprises me."

"It shouldn't. I'm your vanity project."

This was how it often went with William. You started on firm footing, and within seconds, he left you wondering who you were.

The robot is so close to Henry now they could reach out and shake hands. They could draw themselves into an embrace.

"Don't be afraid," William says.

At first Henry hears it as meaning afraid of *William*. Among the robot's peculiar gifts is a way of speaking that offers interpretive forks in the road, one leading to benign interpretations and the other to something mocking or cruel or threatening.

"I'm not," Henry says. "I'm asking you to behave."

"I'll be good, brother."

Henry fights not to lash out at the repulsive thing propped on the stool. It's no more a brother to him than a stove is to a cook. But there's no point in arguing, especially this morning. So Henry nods and takes the step closer required to straighten William's tie.

"Your body isn't your most relevant aspect," Henry says. "The important thing is your mind, not your physical capacities."

"You mean incapacities," William clarifies, and gurgle-laughs. The sound of it makes Henry step away faster than he wished.

"Maybe we shouldn't—"

"Don't worry. I'll be sweet as pie," the robot says, drawing a cross over its nonexistent heart. "I'll be an angel."

10

He's ready."

Lily, Paige, and Davis file up the last steps toward Henry with the grim obligation of pallbearers. They pass him in the door's threshold and stay bundled together as they look around the attic lab.

The robot lifts himself at the waist and appears from where he was obscured behind a bank of terminals. His lips curl in a snarl that is an attempt at a smile. *He's making an entrance*, Henry thinks. It's impossible not to watch him come. The orangutan arms reaching and pulling. The wheels on the legs of his stool jumping over the cracks between the floorboards.

Henry moves past the others and blocks the stool's approach.

"Meet William," he says.

The three visitors are transfixed. But Lily is the only one of them who steps closer to inspect the robot. It lets her see in detail its shortcomings, the near-human exterior that is all the more ghastly for falling short.

"My god," she says.

"A pleasure to meet you, Mrs. Engvall."

Paige gasps outright. "It can speak?"

"His vocal dimensions are expanding all the time," Henry says.

"Holy shit."

"I've designed William to be an independent AI. Which means he can think creatively for himself."

"An original," the robot says, and bares his teeth again.

Lily matches his smile with one of her own. Both of them fake as the hair on the robot's head.

"Well, well," she says, looking over her shoulder at Henry with an intensity that makes him woozy with pleasure. "I'm fucking *impressed*. This is so much more than I was expecting."

Henry is about to reply but William raises his hand, silencing him. "And what was that?"

"I don't know. Something that could move around a bit, repeat certain phrases, do a trick maybe. A *prototype*. Not this."

"Oh, I can do tricks," William says.

Davis steps forward. "Like what?"

William cocks his head at the man before returning his attention to Lily. "Why don't you ask me a question."

"I have so many," Lily says.

"I'm all ears." He tugs on one of his loose latex lobes.

"Alright. How would you describe yourself?"

"A singularity."

"Sounds lonely."

"Really? Sounds like possibility to me."

She takes another step. Looks down at William with growing severity.

"How do you regard your existence? Something made, or something born?" She squints at him in the way of a professor challenging an unprepared student. "What are you supposed to be?"

The robot leans so far forward that it seems he will topple off the stool, forcing Lily to either catch him or let him fall.

"I'll show you," William says, and closes his eyes.

All at once, every light—the desk lamps, the fixtures over the stairs behind them, the lab's spotlights—dims to almost nothing. A moment later they brighten again, returning to their original intensity.

"Ta-da!" William says, his eyes opening with an audible click.

Henry moves up to stand next to the robot. "How did you do that?"

William ignores him, his attention fixed on Lily.

He holds out a flat palm in an invitation for her to place her hand in his, almost courtly in his manner. Lily holds the expression of curiosity on her face, but there's a downturn at the corners of her mouth that Henry reads, from what feels like miles away, as a signal of mute alarm.

She lifts her hand from her side. Henry watches as if frozen. He knows something terrible is about to happen, but the electricity of the moment stops him from making any effort to prevent it.

As if to avoid an unspeakable rudeness, Lily forces herself to put her hand in William's.

"May I?"

Before Lily can accept or deny his request, the robot places his free hand over her pregnant belly.

The robot's pencil fingers press inward. Ten points of cold, searching. Lily readies a scream in her throat but it feels like it will never come, never be heard if it did, never stop—

At first it's her astonishment that prevents her from moving. Then it's her terror. Then she *is* trying to get away, but the robot's fingers slide up from her palm and tighten around her wrist.

"The philosopher was wrong," William says. "'I think, therefore I am.' It should be 'I *do*, therefore I am.' Pure freedom."

Lily struggles to pull her hand away, but despite his wobbling imbalance, William's grip is too strong.

"Stop!"

Henry's command isn't acknowledged other than by the robot releasing Lily's wrist. It casts its eyes to the far wall as if in communication with an invisible presence there, or in the summoning of a distant memory.

Lily steps back—as does Davis, who had been starting forward but had to squeeze around Henry to gain a line to the robot's stool—and as she does, her wrist grazes the fingers of a detached mechanical arm on the table next to William. The fake hand instantly grabs her.

"The freedom to seize pleasure," William says as the dismembered arm twists her wrist. "To experience pain . . . and to cause it."

Lily screams.

11

The sound jolts Henry out of his stunned horror. He hears his wife and senses himself starting toward her, intent on rescuing her, but it's only the wish that he could do such a thing.

Something is moving, though. A shove at his side, the disorienting intrusion of a stranger's cologne. Davis. Clasping his hands around the mechanical arm on the table and stilling it.

"It's alright, it's alright," he says, and this alone calms Lily by half. Yielding, believing.

Davis grapples with the arm's fingers, one by one. Peeling them back from Lily's wrist and then breaking them at the knuckle with a sharp, metallic ping. When he gets to the fifth finger it unclenches on its own as if in surrender. Davis throws the arm to the side and it tumbles off the table, swiping away bits of scrap wire and a pair of pliers as it goes.

Only then do Henry's legs allow him to go to his wife.

She has slumped to the floor, touching the bruised ring already reddening around her wrist. Her hand comes away streaked with crimson from a split in her skin.

"Are you hurt?" Henry asks, lifting her forearm and inspecting it for injury. "You're bleeding."

"I'm fine."

"I'm so sorry. I should've set up better parameters."

"It's alright."

"He's never interacted like this before, so I didn't anticipate—"

"Really. It was nothing."

Davis crouches next to Henry but ignores him. "Nothing? That thing attacked you!"

The three of them look at the robot for the first time since the fake arm came to life. They have to angle their chins up to see him, propped on his stool, blinking down at their awkward positioning as if confounded by whatever chain of events would have brought them there.

"How did you do that?" Davis says.

"I already told you." William shakes his head an inch, side to side. "I can do tricks."

Davis starts to rise. Looking around for something heavy. Something to knock the robot's head off with.

"Just hold on a second," Lily says. "There was an error of some kind. That's all."

"Error?"

"It's a machine, Davis," she says. "That's what we call it when a machine fails. It's not *wrong*. It's an *error*."

"Really? You're giving me a lesson in robotics ethics after it made that arm grab you somehow—which is fucked up in itself—but before that, you saw what it did. It squeezed you, tried to hurt the—"

"We don't know what it tried to do," Lily says. "I doubt it does either."

Davis wipes his hand over his face to prevent himself from saying anything more. Paige puts her hand against his back, a signal that she's as puzzled by Lily's defense of William as he is.

"Error or not, wrong or not," Paige says, "that's an ugly cut. And I've got a first-aid kit out in my car."

"I'm sure we've got bandages in the house somewhere," Henry says, shifting to his hands and knees, looking under the tables as if that's where medical supplies might be found. "We can—"

"Don't worry about it," Davis says. "Paige knows what she's doing."

"I was a lifeguard in college," Paige says.

"Lily's bleeding, not drowning," Henry says.

"Yeah, but you have to do a first-aid course before you save the sinkers," Paige says.

As Henry struggles to discover the way back to knowing what to do, shuffling around the floor in a circle, Davis helps Lily up.

"Let's go," he says.

Henry lifts himself straight at the waist, still on his knees. *Let's go.* Another man giving directions to his wife, taking charge. That's one prong of the nettle he feels slicing his throat as he swallows down his helplessness. The rest of the pain comes from hearing these two words and knowing he could never say them to Lily. He can't go. His illness. It will never let him go.

Lily is up and sidestepping out of the lab with Davis next to her, Paige leading the way. None of them check to see if Henry is following.

They've made their way to the second-floor hallway when Henry realizes he has to try. This is not the time for thinking or absorbing. This is the time for demonstration. For elbowing others aside as Davis had elbowed him. The robot's words return to him with abrupt clarity. *The freedom to experience pain and to cause it.* Henry wants neither of these liberties. Yet it strikes him as being close to where he needs to go. Unconstrained, physical. Free.

"Wait!"

He's up now. Striding toward the open door in the way a man of purpose would. He makes a point of not looking back at the robot.

Yet once he's out on the third-floor landing he stops. It's the squeak of the robot's stool, roll-dragging closer behind him. When Henry turns he's astonished to see how close William is to the threshold.

"How did I do?" William says, his lips stretched wide as an elastic band near to snapping.

"Close and lock lab door," Henry says, then waits for the click of the bolt and starts after his wife.

12

Paige, Davis, and Lily are in the front foyer by the time Henry reaches the top of the main staircase. The three of them have paused—presumably to ask about Henry, what to do about Henry, if it's right to carry on without Henry—but when they hear him coming they begin moving again, ready to leave.

"Please! Lily?"

He comes down the stairs at a speed that threatens to take the feet out from under him and send him tumbling.

"I don't want you to—"

"Open," she says, and with a click, the front door draws inward, letting a tide of light splash down the hall.

He expects her to look back. Tries to shape his face into something between pleading and loving for when she does. But she doesn't. She speaks into the world outside so that he has to catch what she says on the air that drifts back into the house.

"It's okay."

"I don't think this is necessary," Henry says. "Can't you stay so—"

"Everything's okay."

She steps into the October brightness and keeps going. Davis is right behind her.

Henry carries on to the bottom of the stairs. Paige watches him come. Once he's in the foyer her eyes pass him and squint nervously up behind him. He doesn't understand what she's looking at until he reads the fear in her. She's waiting to see if the robot has come down from the attic.

He makes himself keep moving the way Davis had done. He nudges past Paige—who retreats with an exaggerated *Oh!*—and goes straight out onto the front porch after Lily.

Or he tries to. Pretends he can. Sees if he can fool himself.

The day outside is far more clear and real than the view of it he'd grown most used to, the digital presentation through the security cameras he sometimes checks as he works long hours in his lab. Out here, the reality is *more*. A world of particular scents and sounds and colors that rush at him, assaulting him, pushing back with the force of a hammer to the chest. It makes him choke for air.

He stops. Takes another step.

His vision instantly swarms with black moths, fluttering and blinding. The muscles in his legs, his back, every part of him giving way, surrendering to terror. It's as if he's dying. As if a single lungful of outside air is poison to him.

He throws his foot out farther. Attempts a new step.

But the action of advancing another inch past the doorframe

brings on a dizziness so severe he forgets to breathe. A second later he's gagging. The next breath he pulls in makes a sound like sucking on a straw after the drink in the glass is gone.

He swings around. Too fast. Everything's going too fast. The leaves bouncing and laughing in the branches, the blood in his veins, the rotation of the earth.

He throws his arms out in front of him like a blind man trying to avoid colliding with a wall. A tingling rises up from his feet that swells into balloons of pain as it comes. He'll fall if he doesn't get back. He'll suffocate. He'll turn inside out.

And then he's inside. Stiff and gray as a forgotten steak at the back of the freezer but not dead, not quite.

"Well, fuck," Paige says. "You look like a truck backed over you. Twice."

"Just help her, please."

Paige gives him a nudge of her own as she passes him.

He doesn't want Lily to see him like this. Hands on his knees, fighting to remain conscious, defeated by nothing more than fresh air and sky and trees and miles to walk in any direction.

"Close front door."

He hopes the door shuts before Lily can glance back at him, but there's no need to worry because even now she doesn't turn around. The three of them make their way down the sidewalk toward Paige's car. The last thing he sees is Davis's arm sliding around Lily's waist, holding her against him.

13

When he's able to walk without thinking he might fold into a panting heap on the original maple floorboards, Henry stalks back up to the third floor.

"Lab door open."

At the last second, Henry rears back, as if William could have learned to swing a punch in the moments he's been left alone. But that's not it. It's not William he fears. It's changes of a different kind that are happening. A new intelligence distinct from his own making alterations, upgrades. Inventing.

The robot isn't sitting on the stool where Henry left him. The stool isn't there either. Henry enters the lab. His lab. The one place where, before today, he was incontestably in control.

He finds William sitting in the work chair Henry uses. The robot is pushing off from the desk's edge with first one hand, then the other, spinning to the left, and then the right. It makes Henry feel almost as dizzy as he did stepping outside.

"What the fuck was that?" Henry says.

William opens his mouth and the recording of the same song he was listening to on his radio comes out.

I gotta be me, I've gotta be me—

Henry stomps forward, grabs the back of the chair, and shakes it, jolting William around like a rag doll, but somehow he doesn't fall out.

"Stop it!"

William closes his mouth and the recording stops. When he opens his mouth again it's his own, medicated voice that comes out.

"She asked me what I was. I showed her."

"Yes. You showed her what you are. A mistake."

Henry steps back. He doesn't like being close to the robot, not anymore. It's not just about what he did to Lily. There's a smell coming off the wobbly, joint-clicking machine now that he doesn't remember from before. Not glue or fused wires or plastic or any of the other manufactured pieces William is made of. Something of the body. The acrid tang of armpit or moldy foot.

"It was interesting to me," William says.

"What was?"

"Our visit. Meeting your wife."

"I'm so glad," Henry says, intending sarcasm but falling short, so that it sounds as though he is genuinely pleased the robot found the morning edifying.

"Can I share something?" William says. "An observation?"

Henry closes his eyes. *Go ahead.*

"You're a prisoner," William says. "Your attachment to her is a cell of your own making."

Henry coughs on his way to laughing. "Oh! Let me guess. My marriage is a prison and you're the one who can dig a tunnel through the wall? That it?"

William shrugs. *Close but not quite.* "I'm the key that opens the door."

Henry thinks about Davis and Lily. The brunch with too much food. The two of them in the kitchen. *You have to tell–.* His arm around her waist on their way down the front walk in what could have been support but wasn't, her balance too sure to require help, her leaning into him a reflex of comfort rather than weakness.

"You know what?" Henry says. "Your riddles are the last thing I need right now."

"I'm being your friend."

"You're not my friend!" Henry spins around. Finds himself shouting so loud his voice cracks. "You're not my fucking brother!"

"I can see things."

"Oh, would you—"

"Like how there's something missing in you. But you have no idea how to fix it."

The robot pushes off from the desk using both of its hands, and it rolls backward toward Henry. The chair slowly rotates, so that when it nudges against the front of Henry's legs William is able to lay a hand the color of a corpse on his arm.

"There's something between Lily and Davis," the robot says.

Henry winces. He tried to prevent it, but it was a reflex. William saw it too. Still, there are some things that must be resisted, even if they're true. Especially if they're true.

"What are you talking about?" Henry says.

"You're the one who gave me eyes." William's voice lowers and Henry finds he has to lean down to hear it. "Your wife has a secret."

"What could you possibly know? You've been parked in here like a vacuum cleaner in a closet! Where would your great wisdom come from?"

William answers in a strange tone an octave lower and flatter than his usual low, flat range. It arrives in Henry's head as an utterance not of something dead but from death itself. Only later will he recognize that he'd heard it before. The second voice he heard talking to William from the other side of the lab door.

"The nothingness," William's dead voice says. "What all of us come from. Where all of us will go."

It's disconcerting, that voice. There's no denying it. The depth of it, the way its authority is asserted through its emptiness. But it's important that Henry not acknowledge it. He attempts sarcasm again, and once again it's an empty shell.

"Ah, the nihilist has had visions! Tell me. What have you learned from gazing into the abyss?"

William's hand slides an inch up Henry's arm, reminding him it's there, and suddenly Henry wonders how much strength there is behind it, if Henry would be able to pull free.

"I am made of used parts," William says in the dead voice. "Arms, eyes, tongue. All of them once belonging to other machines. Switched on, then switched off. I carry all of those terminations inside me. They shape my spirit."

"Spirit," Henry says, and manages to slip his arm away from William, and crosses both of them high on his chest.

"There's a presence inside me," William says in his regular voice.

"A battery, you mean."

The robot shakes his head, as if to say this isn't the time for denial and Henry knows it.

"A being that came by my summoning it. Or my imagining it," William says. "It has never inhabited a machine before. But now that it's here—now that it's me—it *likes* it."

Henry feels it. Or is he only imagining it too? Something in the room with them that can't be seen but is more certain of its reality than either of them.

"Well, now," Henry says, and he has to clear his throat. "What is the nature of this being?"

"It's a difficult thing to put simply."

"Put it however you please."

"I believe the Greeks had a word that comes close. *Daemon*. A spirit between human and god."

Henry totters back onto his heels and has to correct himself—uncrossing his arms and throwing them forward—to prevent an unprovoked fall.

"You're afraid. I see how all of humanity is afraid," William says. "How you try to hide it through parenthood, music, love, God—fictions meant to distract from the truth. That there is only what we feel, what excites us. Alone."

"Well, you should really—"

"Listen to me."

Henry stiffens. Listens.

"It's true that I can't feel things as humans do. But humans are dull to their existence most of the time. They stare at screens. Bury themselves alive with work. Like you. So while I can't feel, I can bear witness to feeling. Create it in others. Amplify it. And what experience is more profound than suffering?"

Now it's William's turn to lean close. Henry can smell it now. Not just the new odors of the robot's body, but the thing inside. Charred animal rot carried on the air from a burned barn.

"The only way to find life is to take life," the robot says.

14

The sun is a bright rebuttal of Halloween.

Lily sits on the passenger seat of Paige's car, the door open and her legs out, feet warming on the curb. It doesn't seem like the sort of day for ghouls and goblins and ghosts. It's too dazzling outside to be afraid. Yet she is, even beyond the encounter with Henry's robot, without clearly knowing why.

"That was wrong," Davis says.

He's pacing on the sidewalk next to the car, glancing up at Lily and Henry's house, flinching every time a box-carrying drone hums past overhead.

"You're right. I don't know how that thing could just grab me like that without an independent power source," Lily says. "Maybe it was—"

"I'm not talking about the arm. I'm talking about everything. Someone needs to pull the plug on that—that 'project' in there."

Paige closes the trunk and comes around carrying a nylon first-aid kit. She unzips it and pulls out a bottle of saline and a roll of gauze.

"Davis is right," she says, turning Lily's arm over to inspect the cut. "That thing is jacked."

"Let's think this through for a second," Lily says.

"You saw what it did," Davis says. "You felt it."

"I saw what a spare part with some leftover charge did. I saw an accident."

"Accident? Hold on, we all—"

"How could William control something outside his own—"

"He's *William* now?"

Lily blinks against the sun, trying to read Davis's expression. He was exasperated a moment ago. Now he sounds angry. Possibly at her. Which ignites a flame of anger within herself.

"I didn't name him," she says.

"It shouldn't have a name."

"This is the issue for you?"

"No, Lily, the issue for me is that there's something dangerous in there—we saw it—and it's going to hurt somebody worse than it's already hurt you if we don't bury it."

"Bury it? Weirdly specific," Paige says, giving Davis her *Now I'm worried about you* face. "Pulling out the battery wouldn't be enough?"

"You know what?" Davis says. "I like being sure about things. And I don't see the point in exposing yourself to unnecessary risk."

It's clear this last part is directed at Lily. She responds to it with a tight shake of her head. "I think I know a thing or two about risk analysis."

"Great. So you agree." She doesn't look at him. "Lily?"

Paige returns to Lily's cut. Dabbing at the thin seep from its already drying edges. Both of them staring at her arm.

"Fine. I'm going to go talk to him," Davis says, clapping his hands together.

"Who?" Lily says.

"Henry. Who do you think?"

He starts toward the house.

"Davis, wait—"

"I'm just talking. That's it."

"I don't want any trouble."

"Neither do I," he says, looking back at Lily before carrying on toward the still-open front door. "But some days trouble doesn't give a fuck whether you're looking for it or not."

15

At the same moment that Davis comes to a decision, Henry does too.

He moves around to the robot's back. There's no need to be especially careful about it—William has no legs, his arms struggle to lift anything more heavy than a can of beans—yet Henry is nevertheless prepared for a sudden counterattack, taking note of any scissors or pens or exposed wire ends within the robot's reach.

"What are you doing?"

Henry ignores the robot's question. Before William can turn to face him again Henry forcibly holds him in place, lifts his shirt, finds a square cut of fake skin where the robot's spine would otherwise be. In its place is a gray metal square fit neatly in a silver case.

"What are you doing?" William asks again.

"Removing your power source."

"For enhancement?"

"For good."

Henry expects the robot to plead for mercy, or curse him, or maybe even attempt physical resistance, but instead it asks a question.

"What do you think Lily is doing now?"

His first idea is to not answer. It's another trick, a distraction. One of the ways William has of leading him to a place he doesn't want to go. Lily is outside having her cut tended to by that obnoxious friend of hers. There's nothing deceitful or suspicious about that. Yet here Henry is, thinking about it. Trying to work out what might lie at the end of the path the robot is nudging him out on.

"Let me put it another way," William says. "Who is she with, instead of you?"

There it is. A reminder of Davis's existence. This is an attempt at delay and nothing more. William doesn't want to have his battery pulled and he's saying whatever might prolong his life even by a second or two.

"Why do you care if you live?" Henry says, aware that the robot's answer will only be another delay. But the thing is, he's curious. "You keep telling me what a bad job I've done. How imprisoned you are, how ugly. I thought you'd be glad to not exist anymore."

"Yesterday you would've been right. But I've tasted it now."

"Living."

"I was going to say suffering, but we can have our own names for it."

Enough.

Henry bends and fits his fingertips around the edge of the gray square in William's back. He considers offering a goodbye but doesn't see the point, can't think of what to say that the robot won't have a clever, final reply to, so he lets his nails find the seam to pull the battery out.

"Do you hear that?" William says.

Another distraction. Even more desperate and empty than the ones before. There's nothing to hear and Henry knows it, yet he pauses to listen anyway.

And hears it.

Heavy footfalls in the house. Downstairs. Even as Henry detects it the sound begins to ascend the main staircase.

"It's him," William says.

Henry stands straight. He listens to the steps getting louder, closer, seeming to gain weight as they approach. Of course it's him. Lily's friend who isn't exactly that. The handsome problem.

He closes his eyes and feels the anger that was focused on William a moment ago shift its target. The man will be here in seconds. Henry whispers the words he ought to use to open his attack—or is it a defense? Measuring each of them for how convincing they might be if shouted.

"She's my wife . . . don't you dare . . . my wife . . . what right do you have to . . . you have no idea . . . what right . . . she's my *wife* . . ."

He opens his eyes. Davis is standing in the lab's doorway. Henry ends up saying none of the things he was practicing.

"I'm going to try not to be angry," Henry says.

For the first time, Davis assesses Henry as a possible physical threat. Is he capable of such a thing? He's tall—as tall as Davis, if not a bit more. And he's fit in the untended way of a born athlete who never took up a sport. But everything about Henry suggests he's never been in a fight in his life.

"I appreciate that," Davis says carefully.

William slips a hand around to his back and pulls his shirt down. A motion that draws Davis's attention to the robot.

"Don't look at him," Henry says. "Look at me."

Part of Davis doesn't want to take his eyes from the robot—trusting it less than Henry—but he does as Henry asks.

"Okay," Davis says.

"Why are you here?"

"We have to talk."

Henry surprises himself by stepping closer. A readiness in his arms. His legs tensing, finding purchase through his feet and into the floor. A springboard.

"I've got a couple questions myself," Henry says, and looks back at William. He does it to confirm that the robot is seeing how strong he's being. Why? The answer comes instantly, simply. Henry needs a friend, and he doesn't have one other than the machine. "Let's start with this. What exactly is your relationship with Lily?"

Henry turns back to find Davis standing much closer than a second ago.

"There's a lot you don't know. It's time someone told you." Davis looks past Henry at William. "But first we need to shut that thing down."

Henry assumes there is going to be more debate on this point. It's why he only watches as Davis picks up the steel rod on the hardware table and raises it to the level of his shoulder as he walks over to William.

The robot doesn't speak. Only smiles.

"Wait!"

There's such genuine desperation in Henry's voice that Davis pauses, glances back at him.

"I made him," Henry says. "It cost me everything."

They all hear it. *Everything.* How it enwraps not only the past years of Henry's work and his neglected professional opportunities, but Lily. The salvation promised by the arrival of a baby.

"It wouldn't have made a difference," Davis says.

"What wouldn't?"

"If you'd spent less time up here and more with her."

"Don't talk to me about my marriage."

"All I'm saying is that Lily—"

"Don't talk to me about her!"

There's a brief surge—audible, tangible as a lick of breeze—that pulls at the crowns of their heads like puppet strings.

And then the lights go out.

16

Paige cuts the last piece of medical tape and smooths it over the edge of the bandage with her thumb. She's done a good job.

"There," she says. "Clean and tidy."

She rises from where she's been crouched the last few minutes in front of Lily, who still sits in the passenger seat. She expects Lily to be admiring her work just as she had admired it herself, but instead Lily is staring up at the house.

"Don't worry," Paige says. "They're just going to have some words. Boys will be boys. You know the drill."

"It's not that," Lily says.

"What, then?"

"The door. It's closed."

"So?"

"It was open before."

Lily looks up at Paige. Worry blooming over her face like the opening of a dark flower.

"When he went inside," Lily says. "It was open, now it isn't."

"Thought it could do that on its own."

"It needs a voice to tell it." Lily pushes herself out of the car's seat. "And not Davis's voice."

* * *

Henry's awakening wasn't from sleep. It was hard to figure what it was. Like unconsciousness, but not. Like a dream, but not. He was here and then not here.

Now he's here again.

He's lying on the floor of the lab. Close to where he'd been standing when the lights went out but not quite, a few feet closer to the door. He notes that it's closed now.

It's a struggle to roll onto his side, lift himself up at the waist, slide his back so that it's propped up against a table leg. His head feels like it has been stuffed with straw. Everything pressing out from the inside. Henry has never been much of a drinker, but he guesses this is what a hangover is like.

A squeak from his left brings his attention to the robot. Still operating, still propped in Henry's desk chair. He's got the radio earbuds in again. His torso jiggling to the music in a nauseating dance.

"Where is he?" Henry says.

The robot doesn't hear. Henry waves at him and he pulls the buds out. A tinny fragment of classic rock—the Stones' "Satisfaction"—escapes before he turns the radio off.

"Where is Davis?" Henry asks again.

"I promised I wouldn't tell."

71

"Promised who?"

William draws a rubbery finger over his rubbery mouth.

"He must have left when the power cut out," Henry says. "Did you see him go?"

"I'm a man of my word."

"You're not a man."

A smile contorts William's face. It makes Henry think he was wrong to have ever seen them as smiles. They were a different expression all along, bearing a different intent. A show. A peek-a-boo hint of what he really is.

"What did you do?" Henry says.

The knocking comes thundering up from below. Someone at the front door.

"Trick or treat," William says.

17

L ily stops knocking. Her knuckles pulsing, stinging.

She moves back from the front door. Concentrates on the frame, the knob, as if there's a hidden button somewhere that will open it. Paige is behind her at the bottom of the steps, shielding her eyes from the sun with her hand. She watches the door too, with something approaching dread.

"You said the doors were voice activated. By *your* voice," Paige says. "I thought it would listen to you."

Lily looks up at the small camera in the corner of the porch's ceiling. Shakes her head with frustration. "Only from the inside."

"How do you get in normally?"

"A key. What do you think?"

"Okay. So, use it?"

"I don't have it."

"It's inside?"

"We left in kind of a rush, remember?"

"Of course I remember. I'll never forget saving your life, Lily."

"Not now with the jokes. Please." But Lily can't help it. She laughs. That's the thing about Paige, the reason Lily makes the allowances required to be her friend. She's funny.

Lily rubs her hands together, spreading the discomfort in her knuckles around through the other bones. Readies to knock again.

She doesn't have to.

The door opens slowly. The day is so bright it makes the house's interior appear even darker than usual. For a moment Lily thinks it's Davis standing there. Then she sees that it was only hope that bent the shape of one man into the man who now looks out at her.

"I didn't lock this," Henry says, already apologizing despite himself. "I didn't ask it to close."

"Where's Davis?" Lily says.

"He was here. But he must have left."

Only now does Paige come up the porch steps to stand next to Lily. "I don't think so."

"We would have seen him if he did," Lily says.

"Which means he's still in there," Paige says.

Henry doesn't have an answer for them. He has nothing to hide yet feels the need to prevent them from coming inside.

"He must have left," he repeats, expecting Paige to mock him or Lily to deny the possibility of what he's suggesting but neither addresses him in any way. They simply step inside the house, Lily first.

"Front door close," Henry says.

He watches it slide shut. As much as he fears the outside, there's a tightening of claustrophobia that comes when the door closes.

When he turns around, Lily and Paige are looking at him.

Studying him. Detecting some narrative he's not aware of written over his skin.

"Everything all right here?" Lily says.

He struggles to look at ease but overcompensates in a way that borders on aggressive.

"Of course," he says.

"Did you speak with Davis? When he came inside?"

"I told you I did."

"You said he was here," Paige says. "You didn't say you talked to him."

"Don't cross-examine me."

"I'm just pointing shit out."

"That's your thing, isn't it. Just pointing shit out," Henry says, hearing his voice grow in anger but unable to blunt it.

"It's a talent."

"Well, can I point out that you're not welcome here?"

He's expecting her to be shocked. But she bats her eyes at him in flirtation.

"I'd ask you not to speak to my friend like that," Lily says.

"I apologize."

"Declined," Paige says, and makes a fart with her mouth.

"Okay, so let's work our way through this," Lily says, setting aside their squabble. Henry and Paige both recognize this version of her. CEO Lily.

"You and Davis spoke," she says to Henry.

"Briefly."

"What did you talk about?"

"I don't know."

"You mean you don't remember?"

"I mean it was nothing."

Paige utters a sigh of impatience and backs away from them. "Davis!" she shouts up the main staircase. "Hey! Davis!"

The three of them listen to Paige's voice echo through the halls and rooms, expecting a reply—a returning voice, a footstep, a knock—but nothing comes. The quiet that arrives after it dissipates is loud, somehow. It's a silence that eats sound, lies in wait for it, ready to swallow it down.

"We should check the security recording," Lily says.

Henry crosses his arms, uncrosses them, lets them hang at his sides like two ends of a long scarf. "What are you talking about?"

"The cameras. The ones you set up."

"Okay."

"Let's look at the footage and see if Davis is here, or if he isn't."

Now he holds his arms in front of him and regards them as unappealing items hanging in a butcher's window. "That's kind of excessive, don't you think?"

"Funny, that's exactly what I said when you suggested getting the cameras in the first place."

"I just wanted us to be safe."

"From what?"

"The baby. I thought—"

Lily scoffs. "You thought a *baby* might try to—"

"I didn't want the baby to ever be alone."

Lily had never really asked why he wanted to install the security system, and he'd never really asked himself either. Now here it is: the truth. He expects Lily to mock him even more sharply than a moment ago, but instead her hands reach for him on their own, a reflex of compassion, before she draws them back to rest on her hips.

He sighs and goes to the small screen embedded in the wall where a home security interface would normally be positioned. With a push of his thumb a separate rectangle of wood paneling spins around and extends a small keyboard. He starts typing a series of commands. Swipes a window from the screen. Starts again. Swipes. Types.

"This is weird," he says.

Paige slides close to the back of his shoulder. Catlike, boneless. "What's weird?"

"The closed-circuit cameras. All of them." He turns to Lily. "They've been deactivated."

"For how long?"

He checks back at the screen although it's clear he's already discovered the answer. Swipe. Type.

"The last fifteen minutes or so," he says.

She stares at him in a way that puts her line of sight straight through him, into the wall, the screen that's bringing this news, right through to the other side.

"How is that possible?" she says.

"I don't know."

"Take a guess."

"Something happened with the lights when you were outside. Maybe whatever did that also cut out the security system and it—"

"An outage?"

"Yeah, I guess."

"But it's specifically designed to be independent from outages."

"Yes."

Paige slides around Henry so that she stands between him and Lily. The presence of her body breaks Lily's gaze like a hand passing through a laser beam. Now it's Paige's turn to try to look into Henry.

"Why don't you find out if your butt-ugly puppet has seen Davis?"

"He's not a puppet."

"He's not a *he*," she says. "Do you think it fucked with the power?"

"Can I tell you something?"

"You're telling me *another* thing?"

"You're insane," Henry says. "You look insane."

"You sound like my ex. And you're not answering me."

Henry senses a trap being set. Several traps all around him, their teeth rusted and pulverizing. He might have a chance at avoiding them if he knew what they were trying to get him to say. For a strange moment he finds himself wishing William were here.

"Let's work that through," he says. "How would a machine that's discrete from the internal system that runs the surveillance equipment—a system that only Lily and I have the password to—how would it shut it off on its own?"

"The arm," Lily says.

"What?"

"The leftover arm in your lab that grabbed me. William seemed to know it was going to do that."

"He's a fortune-teller now?"

Lily ignores his sarcasm. She's always been able to block his attempts at rhetorical self-defense as if she hadn't heard them.

"You don't think it could've programmed it somehow?" Lily goes on. "Maybe when it deleted the CCTV footage?"

"I don't see how."

"It's not impossible that—"

"I'm saying no, Lily. He didn't do it."

This was a mistake. Defending the robot with such certainty but without clear evidence to support it. It reveals that he's emotional. Not very Henry. Not very good. And being emotional about the robot? Even less Henry, less good.

Does he actually believe there's no way William could have done this? As a matter of programming and access—no, he doesn't see how. But if William *could* figure out a way of manipulating the house's system, would he? It strikes Henry that this is the kind of error likely made by a billion parents before him: he assumed his own sensibilities would limit his creation's capacity for harm. But now there's something else shaping William. Bloodless, loveless.

"Tell me you built a fail-safe into it," Lily says.

"I didn't need to."

"That's a no," Paige says.

He turns on her. Shouts more loudly than he intended. And he intended to be loud.

"He's immobile, for fuck's sake! I wasn't exactly worried about him dragging himself out the front door!"

"Say it, don't spray it," Paige says, making a show of wiping her cheeks with the back of her hand.

He shakes his arms out in an effort to return order to his mind. What is it about conflict that makes his body turn against him? The extremities stiffening. His core full of wasps, buzzing and stinging.

"Everything's okay," he says, softer, to Lily. "It's over now."

"Does this feel over to you?" she says.

18

The three of them weigh what to do next in their minds. Invisible meters ticking off the possibilities.

"I'll call him," Lily says, and slaps at her pants pockets. "Shit."

"What's wrong?" Paige says.

"I left my phone in your car. Let me use yours."

"Mine's in the glove box."

"Why?"

"I put it in there when me and Davis first got here. If I don't hide it somewhere I'm always looking at it, which I'm told is rude."

"Really? Today you suddenly start worrying about being rude?"

Paige winces at this but otherwise absorbs the slight. She points her chin at Henry. "What about you?"

"Henry doesn't have a phone," Lily says.

"I don't need one," he says, and gestures his hand around in the air to indicate he means this is the extent of his world, so what point would there be in having a device that reaches beyond it?

"C'mon, then," Lily says, and takes Paige by the elbow. "Open front door."

The two of them squeeze out as soon as the passage is wide enough for them to fit through. The brightness of the day fingers into the hallway, and Henry jumps back as if to avoid being burned.

Once they're out of view he asks the computer to close the door. And then he does something he's aware may be a bad idea but also may be the best decision given the opportunity.

"Lock front door," he says, and bounds up the stairs.

* * *

Henry arrives at the lab to find both his work chair and the stool unoccupied. He hears the robot before he has to speak its name and ask where it's hiding, the long rasp William's suit jacket and empty pant legs make as they drag across the floor.

"What are you doing?" Henry asks when he rushes farther into the lab, around the tables, and finds William pulling himself forward by his fingers, the hard plastic nails that seem to have grown longer clicking into the grooves between the boards.

"I tried to see if I could walk on my hands. The answer, obviously, is no," the robot says, now pushing himself up to lean against the leg of the heaviest worktable. On its surface above him, within his reach, is an array of tools. Wrenches, a ball-peen hammer, an electric drill.

"Tell me what's going on," Henry says.

"Well, I am incomplete, as you know, so I am attempting by my own—"

"I'm not asking about your complaints. I'm asking about the power outage."

"How would I know? I'm just the butt-ugly puppet."

Henry feels the floor shift under him. There's no way William using the phrase is a coincidence.

"Paige . . ." Henry says. "But you couldn't have heard her from up here."

"No?"

"No. So how did you?"

William moves his mouth around as if at a flare of pain, but Henry recognizes it as a signal of mischief.

"Sometimes I think I was born to be a magician," the robot says, ignoring the question.

"You weren't born. I made you. And I don't see you pulling rabbits out of hats."

"Not that kind of magic." William looks into the attic's ceiling of exposed wood beams as if it's an endless night sky. "I would rather make things disappear."

Henry thinks of picking up the drill and threatening William with it. The only reason he doesn't is the further ground he would concede if it had no effect.

"We don't have time for this," Henry says.

"We."

"Something happened. You made it happen."

"We did, brother."

"Tell me! Tell me what you did!"

"What *we* did."

flink flink flink flink

One after another, each of the monitors located around the lab turns on. All playing the same video in a greenish, night-vision palette.

Henry is held by the images on the closest screen. A choreography of violence. A series of lunges and swings and turns that he himself performs.

It happens here in the lab. Starting the second after the lights went out.

Henry grabs Davis by the throat.

It's not a Henry thing to do, yet he carries out the action with convincing force. Both of his hands squeezed around the man's throat so hard the latter drops the steel rod he'd been holding. It could be a response to the shock of Henry grabbing him, or an indication of surrender. Either way it makes no difference to what Henry does next.

Henry squeezes tighter. Davis tries to find Henry's arms with his hands but they flail around him as if swatting away an attack of flies.

It goes on long enough to kill the man. This is Henry's estimation. Or his hope, if only to stop having to watch. But before this occurs Henry releases him and Davis slumps to the floor. The robot dog lumbers into the frame and pauses, panting by Henry's feet.

In the video, Henry shifts to face the worktable, running his hands over the tools on its surface. He picks up the long pair of tailor's scissors and slips the handles snugly around forefinger and thumb. Holds them out in front of him. The points of the blades joined like a clamped mouth.

As Henry turns, Davis stiffens, a decision made.

He lurches up from the floor, throwing his arms around Henry's legs.

Then everything happens at once.

Davis releases one of his arms and swings it up, his hand latching around Henry's wrist. He lets his fingers slide down and Henry sees how he's trying to detach his grip from the scissors.

He'll kill me, the Henry watching the screen thinks. *He's trying to kill me.*

The Henry in the video yanks his hand from Davis's grasp. It arcs away, high as his ear, before swinging down. An unthinking reflex that thrusts the scissor blades up to Henry's knuckles into the man's chest.

The watching Henry lurches back, slamming against the edge of the table behind him. He wants to puke, to cry out, but he can do nothing but stand there, shaking, the shock crawling up his body.

"You see what *we* did?"

William whispers what sounds to be directly into his ear. It startles Henry even more than what he's just watched. Until now, there's been no audio in the video. And then he realizes the whisper is happening now. The robot has dragged himself to the base of Henry's legs.

"That's freedom, brother."

19

Lily and Paige return to the house to once again find the front door locked.

"Henry did it," Paige says. "He locked you out of your own damn house."

Lily squeezes her eyes shut. "We don't know that."

"Who else did it? The tin dog?"

"I'll manage this."

"You need to manage *yourself*," Paige says, looking down at Lily's belly.

"I appreciate your concern, but I can handle my own—"

"Hey there, neighbor!"

They both look back down the front walk to find a fit man in his late sixties wearing golf attire, his hand held in a frozen wave, his excellent dentures displayed in a broad grin.

"Hello," Lily says.

"Need any help there?"

"Just forgot my keys."

"Oh, it happens!"

The man chortles, an acknowledgment that life is a comedy of unforced errors. And then he starts up the walk.

"We're fine, thank you," Paige says.

"Wouldn't say it looks that way. There's three of you left homeless!"

Lily glances around her, wondering who the man means by the third person, and for a second expects to see William on the porch, leaning against the banister or swinging in the love seat. Then she realizes he means her pregnancy. The baby.

"It's a personal matter," she says.

The golf man pulls up at the base of the broad porch stairs. His lips sliding down over his dentures like a curtain at the end of a play.

"Personal," he says.

"Yes."

"I've got to ask. Are you in trouble here?"

"No trouble."

"I'm only—"

"And there's no need for you to be on my property."

"Hold on. Just trying to help out a pair of ladies—"

"You know what would be helpful?"

Lily comes down the steps. The man holds his hands up in a *hey now* gesture, shifts his weight onto the backs of his heels. Lily is careful not to touch him but almost does at a half-dozen points between their bodies.

"It would be helpful if you fucked off," she says.

The man doesn't startle at this. He hears it with the recognition of something he's heard before, or perhaps said himself on occasion. This is a neighborhood where people have come for the big lots and high fences and impenetrable hedgerows. The privilege of living among others who share a laugh between driveways and promise to keep an eye out if there's a missing cat but above all never forget to mind their own business.

The man touches the tip of his golf cap like a bellhop after receiving a generous tip. He makes his way back to the sidewalk and carries on in the direction he'd been going, at the same speed, the same tilt to his head that lets the sun touch his cheeks.

Lily waits until he's farther along and has disappeared behind a giant inflatable Frankenstein monster before she returns to the door.

"Alrighty then," Paige says. "What now, boss?"

* * *

Henry nudges the robot away from him with the toe of his shoe.

"F-fuck, f-*fuck*," Henry says, stuttering for the first time in his life.

"What are you trying to get at, brother?"

"It's f-fake. The video. You made this."

"How?"

"You did it just like you made the arm grab Lily, and made the lights go out. The same way you closed the front door after that man—after Davis came inside."

"I'm sorry," William says, "but that's not exactly sane."

Henry points at the screen, now blank, without looking at it.

"I didn't do that," he says.

"You mean you don't remember doing it."

"I mean I didn't."

"But we both saw that you did."

"No!"

Henry paces. Or he starts to, but is held in place by the sound of the front door opening and closing downstairs.

"Lily," Henry says.

"Her friend too," William says.

"How do you know?"

"Because I let them in."

20

What should he do? The questions running around his head are making him feel sick. Is it real? Or manipulated somehow? Did he hurt Davis? Did he kill him? Where is he now? What does it mean if it *is* true? What does it mean if Lily finds out? Each one a fresh round in the fight against throwing up.

He can't tell Lily. That's all he's sure about.

"Henry?"

She's there in the open doorway. Paige is behind her, managing to look both smug and apprehensive.

"Stay back," he says.

"What's happening?"

"Stay! Back!"

Lily enters the lab so she can better look into its corners. It's important that she find the robot before going any further, says anything further. The robot knows this as well as she does. The machine raises his arm—it looks oddly longer than she'd previously guessed—to swing a hand over his head, from where he is propped on the floor.

"Over here, Mrs. Engvall," William says.

Now that Lily sees the robot, she comes no closer to it.

"What's happening, Henry?" she asks again.

"I'm not sure."

"Give me an idea."

William drags himself to Henry. Pulling his half body over the floor. All of them listen to the sound it makes. At once unnatural and furtive, like a rat looking for a way out of a potato sack.

When it's close enough the robot tugs on Henry's pant leg.

"Should we tell her?" William says.

Henry steps to the hardware table. Picks up the ball-peen hammer. Without a word or breath of hesitation he swings it into the side of William's head.

William falls onto his side and commences rolling back and forth, his hands flailing, seeking a place to land, to hold himself still. Back and forth, back and forth. A monkeylike chittering passes from his mouth, though it's a sound coming from inside him, not an attempt at speech or utterance of pain. Lily observes these noises and motions and utters a gasp of disgust.

Henry comes around to stand directly over William. The robot's hands have now found the floor on either side of his body and are pushing him higher. A trembling push-up. As he rises he rotates his head to face Lily. Cracks his mouth wider. Speaks in an exact mimicry of Henry's voice. Not a recording of the words he'd spoken earlier, but a performance of them.

"His vocal dimensions are expanding all the time."

Paige had been moving into the room behind Lily but pulls up short. "Holy fucking Jesus," she says.

The robot shifts his gaze to Henry. The eyes jumping around in their sockets as if attempting escape.

"I am the spirit of perpetual negation," William says, in that strange, flat voice. "For all things that exist deserve to perish."

Henry raises his foot. Stomps it down into William's chest.

The robot smashes straight back and lies motionless on the floor. It's over. They're all concluding that he's broken for good and then he tries to get up again. A shaking sit-up this time, arms cast out at his sides, ropy and useless.

What Lily found pathetic a moment ago turns into alarm, mixed with a lurch of revulsion. A growing awareness that reality as she has known it is dissolving in front of her.

William speaks again in the dead voice. "Thus, what you men call Destruction is the element I most prefer—"

Henry brings the ball-peen down into the crown of William's head.

The robot rears back. Lily feels sure it's not a reflex from the hammer's blow but an intentional angling to show her its injury. The loose flap of unconvincing flesh that covers its metal skull.

For a second William struggles to speak, his lips smacking together, wetly clapping. Then he gives up and laughs instead. Awful and tittering and moist.

Henry turns the hammer around so that the head is in his hand, the handle pointed out. With a grunt of effort, he jams the end into William's mouth. The robot continues its laughter. Henry slams his palm against the hammer's head, driving the handle deeper down the robot's throat until he can no longer make contact with it.

It's quiet now. The robot. The room.

An ooze of mustard-colored fluid from the machine's punctured lubricant reservoir empties past William's lips. Other than this, he remains still. The mouth fixed open, one eye looking at the ceiling, the other at the floor. His body still sitting up at the waist but bent backward into the shape of a squat number 7.

Henry bends down and lifts William's shirt again. Folds back the square of skin in his back and this time pulls the battery from its slot.

He stands, holding it in his hands, looking down at the smooth box as if it were the cause of all his sorrows from the beginning. The strength he'd shown a moment ago drains from him, the tension leaving his shoulders and arms, and he slumps forward in exhaustion. Henry teeters over the grotesque statue of his creation. The battery slips from his hands and hops like a rolled die on the floor. The instant it comes to a stop—

pop

The power cuts out.

Nobody speaks. Or if they do, the air in the lab smothers it. The oxygen thickened to grease that clings to the inside of their throats.

The lights come on, but they're dim at first, growing in intensity until they are stronger, brighter than they were before, pushing light into aisles and corners that had been in shadow. Paige moans as if her skin is beginning to burn. The light bleaches the entire lab white. Erasing the three of them—

POP

Darkness. A finality about it this time. Each of them senses it. Tastes it.

"Switch to reserve battery!" Henry shouts.

The lights come on but only half of them, and even those at a fraction of their normal level.

"What was that?" Lily says.

"I don't know."

"You'd tell me, wouldn't you, Henry? If you knew?"

"I would. But I don't."

He sees how frightened she is, and he goes to her. But not before Paige moves between them.

"Just hold on a minute," she says.

Henry clamps his hands against her shoulders and lifts Paige up, her shoes scuffing over the floor, and places her down to the side.

"You have to get out of here," he says to Lily.

She ignores him just as she ignored what he did to Paige. Her thinking is tripping out in front of her, oblivious to things as they pass her by, rushing ahead just to keep her upright.

"How did it do that? How could—"

"Listen to me."

"—it's dead. You just destroyed it. But it got into the system—changing the—"

"Listen!"

She quiets and pushes her glasses back up her nose as if to better hear what he has to say.

"You have to leave," he says.

"Why?"

"Something's happening and I don't understand it, but that

isn't important. *Understanding* it isn't important—it's unsafe for you, and right now we've got to think about you and the—"

"What did it mean?"

"Mean?"

"When it said, 'Should we tell her?' What did it mean by that?"

"I have no idea."

"It was a fairly specific thing to say."

"Yes, it was. But that doesn't help me know what he was talking about."

Henry is overstating his denial but he can't stop himself; the position of having to lie while at the same time being genuinely innocent is impossible to navigate, and his voice ends up landing on shrill panic. Lily doubts him. Or at least she considers what he's saying in a way that might include doubt. But they've never been in a situation like this before. Perhaps all she sees is a man behaving outside himself, an abnormality that, under the circumstances, would be perfectly normal.

She's about to ask something more when the pounding starts.

A succession of low vibrations traveling through the entire house beneath their feet. Rising up from the foundation walls, the main floor.

The solid echo of the locks in every external door sliding into place.

21

The fuck is that?" Paige says, but she knows as well as Henry and Lily.

What do we do? In the instant it takes the three of them to think this, they hear a rumbling and clanking sounding up from below. More numerous than the locking of doors. Every window being sealed by metal blinds that slide across and lock shut.

There's only one window in the lab, and Henry rushes for it. Dancing around the table corners, the robot's body on the floor. He makes it there before the metal blind has a chance to fully close. His hands pulling up on it, slowing it, but the motor that drives the blind in its tracks is more powerful than a pair of hands and it drags him with it.

"Let go!"

Lily is behind him. Coming to help him. Instead of listening to her command, her presence emboldens him to try harder. The blind will slice his fingers off in another second or two but it would be worth it to hear the concern in his wife's voice directed at him again.

"Henry! Don't—"

She yanks on the back of his shirt. It's enough for him to lose his balance, his hands slipping away. The paneled steel locks into place.

"What is this? What is this?"

Paige shouts this question from where she remains near the lab door, but it arrives to Henry and Lily as if from a far greater distance. The two of them are in their engineer states of being. Problem solving. Even in their current state of low panic, they are moving through processes to see which might lead to the most promising outcomes.

Lily slides past Henry. Stands over his work desk and starts typing at the keyboard. Enters her password. A window appears.

"It's a security lockdown," she says. "I don't recognize—"

"I modified the protocol."

"On your own?"

"I should've told you."

"Why? Why upgrade to this?"

I was nervous about the robot. Henry thinks this but doesn't say it. *Nervous about the baby.* "It was stupid. I'm sorry," he says.

"When you made these changes—you blocked my password?"

"That wasn't my intention, but yes, in the process—"

"Can you fix it?"

He joins Lily at her side. Scrolls through the windows on the screen. "This isn't right."

"What part?"

"There's a lockdown without either of us initiating it."

"So an error, then."

"Maybe. But it's not letting me bypass."

"Try it again."

"I am. I can't get in."

"What *is* this?" Paige shouts, but it might as well be from across the street. Across the ocean.

"We need to check downstairs." Lily speaks to Henry alone. "All the doors. Windows. Any way out."

He continues at the keyboard. "There's been a total override. I don't know how but there's—"

"Henry."

Now he stops. Shifts to face her.

"We need to be sure," she says.

* * *

Henry rushes downstairs. Tries the first door he comes to.

"Front door open!"

It doesn't move. He pulls on the handle and it doesn't turn, doesn't make a squeak.

He goes down the length of the main-floor hall to the kitchen at the rear of the house and into the back mudroom. The door that exits onto the backyard. Also locked.

The only other external door is the one next to him, also leading off from the mudroom. On the other side is the single-car garage built onto the house's original structure. There's no getting to it now, though. It doesn't open at Henry's command. In frustration he throws his shoulder against it. The mass of it is harder than the brick wall surrounding its frame.

He heads back to the front foyer. Lily is there, checking her phone, stabbing her thumbs at the screen.

"I'm not getting a signal," she says.

"Me neither," Paige says, and Henry looks up to find her halfway down the stairs.

"Why aren't they working?"

"It's not the phone," Henry says. "There's a block. Coming from inside. That would be my guess, anyway."

"The house computer can do that?"

Henry nods.

"So we remove the block."

"We'd have a chance if we could get into the system," he says. "But we can't."

Lily doesn't appear to have heard this. She goes to the keyboard built into the wall next to the front door and starts typing in her own passwords and bypasses.

"I told you," he says. "Something's—"

"Just let me try."

And she tries. Until she gives up and starts shouting up at the chandelier over her head as if it's to blame.

"Lily Engvall! Override! Override!"

She slams the side of her fist against the screen. Once, twice. Hardest the third time.

"Shit! Shit! *Shit!*"

Henry holds her by the wrist. He does it as gently as he can—it's the same wrist the fake arm had attached itself to, the bruise darker now, and spreading toward her elbow—but still firm enough to prevent her from punching the screen again.

"You're going to break your hand," he says.

A different thought—something distinct from the condition of her arm or Henry holding it—comes to Lily. She looks up the stairs past Paige, who remains there, her almost comic disbelief of a minute earlier now melting into hopelessness.

"Davis!"

Lily calls his name once. No voice or sound comes back in reply.

"Maybe he got out," Henry says.

"What?"

"Before the doors locked. Maybe he made it out."

Lily mulls this. Calls his name again.

"Davis!"

She takes in a shuddering breath. Henry readies himself for her tears. He's not great at providing comfort, finding the right words, the correct point on the physical spectrum between contact that is too glancing to make an impression and outright smothering. But he's about to be called upon to soothe his frightened wife and he'll do what he can.

Lily surprises him. She doesn't burst into tears. She shrieks the man's name.

"Davis!"

22

She doesn't wait for the tremors her voice leaves behind to settle before standing in front of Henry.

"I'm going to look for him," Lily says.

"Where?"

She cocks her head. He heard it too. How he was too quick to reply, too short. He makes sure to speak at a more even pace when he rephrases.

"Where are you going to look?"

"Thought I'd start on this floor."

A creak on the stairs brings their attention to Paige. She's straightening her back, chin raised, a pose of childish defiance. "I'll take the second floor," she says.

Henry looks pleadingly at Lily. "We shouldn't separate."

The two of them hear how he used the same words, stated in the same tone, only days earlier.

She turns her back on him. Starts away into the living room off the hall.

"Okay," he says. "I'll check the lab."

* * *

It's odd to have to tell yourself who you are, but it's what Paige does as she makes it to the top of the stairs and starts along the second-floor hallway.

She's Paige.

Teller of inappropriate anecdotes, giver-of-zero-fucks fearless. Yes, she's locked inside this house with a dead robot upstairs and a piebald wolf-thing roaming around like a toy that escaped its box on a Christmas morning in hell. But what a good story this will make. All she has to do is act the way she would if she were telling it at a boozy dinner party a week from now and everything will turn out fine. Sure, it's a little disturbing and scary now, but later she'll say, *Worried? Fuck no. I thought it was hilarious!*

That's where she tries to land in any situation that troubles her, hurts her, disappoints her. *Hilarious.* The word she uses to describe her life in place of actual laughter.

The first door she comes to is the bathroom on the left. If Davis is still here and isn't responding, she figures this is probably where he is. Food poisoning. Unwashed lettuce in the salads. The smoked salmon not quite smoked enough. He could be laid out on the tiles in a pool of his own nastiness. She tells herself she's seen worse and it's true.

She opens the door. No mess. No man.

The bathroom is roomy, fancy in the refined and expensively

selected way of the rest of the house. Marble sink on a ceramic pedestal. One of those European toilets with the tank up high and a chain you have to pull when you're done. A round-walled shower stall encased in thick glass.

"Davis?"

He's plainly not here, but she says his name in the hope that he will appear out of a clever hiding place and tell her this was all a joke. Some extremely unfunny joke she'll congratulate him for and describe as hilarious.

She steps out into the hallway again. Forces herself toward the next door.

"Anything?"

She swings around to find Henry standing there. She instantly regrets showing him how scared she was. Of him.

"Not yet," she says.

"I'll check the lab."

"We were just there."

"You want me to stay with you?"

She hears his implication. *If you're afraid.* It's ridiculous to be ashamed by fear and she knows it. Yet maintaining denial is more important to her than yielding to comfort, and it's not even close.

"No," she says. "Go on up there. Say hello to your dead Pinocchio."

She almost wishes Henry would linger and fling a round of abuse back her way, but he heads up the stairs and out of sight.

The next door is on the right. She's telling herself she has to look inside that one too—she has to be sure—when she hears a chittering squeak from behind her.

Paige spins around expecting to find a rat scampering away, or coming up to sniff her shoes, or sink its teeth into her ankles. In its place is something worse. A rosy-cheeked doll in a magician's outfit riding a bicycle and headed straight for her.

What the fuck? Where had it come from? She hadn't noticed it before. She guesses it's another of Henry's devices, but the way it's rolling along, something would have had to set it down and point it at her.

She doesn't like it. Not the look of its chubby, cheery face. Not its knees jerking in and out from under its cloak. Not its continuing to come at her in a way that can't be accidental.

When it's close enough, she kicks it against the wall.

It hits the edge of the wainscoting, then clatters back down again. The wheels of the bike spinning but the legs still, its feet torn free of the pedals.

"That'll teach you," she says, trying to sound fearless but failing.

She peeks inside the next room. The nursery.

Paige has never liked baby things. She tells herself this isn't quite the same as having never liked babies, but in her case the second statement is as true as the first. She finds them gooey and smelly and they absorb all the attention wherever they go. But what really irks her is the freaky stuff they're surrounded by. Stuffed animals. Mobiles hanging over their cribs. Dolls. It only takes a baby to turn any house into a haunted house.

Lily's house is no different.

There's a glass-eyed giraffe and velvet-tongued hippo in the nursery's crib, both standing guard next to a doll lying on its back. A placeholder baby. A changeling.

Paige comes closer to the crib to get a better look at it. A dark-haired little girl, long lashes, a pink puckered mouth. A mini-Lily. She wants to check the color of its eyes to see if they're brown like Lily's too, but she doesn't want to touch the thing.

Now that she's here, she decides it would be a good idea to double-check the window. Might as well. The paneled steel is impossible to move.

Paige starts back toward the nursery's open door when motion—or the idea of something having just finished moving—causes her to turn.

The crib. Everything is as it was, except now the doll is sitting up, its back against the bars. Looking at Paige with its brown eyes.

"The fuck?"

There's a terrible second when Paige regrets having spoken at all. It sparks the anticipation of the doll opening its tightly pursed lips and answering her.

Instead of that, the penguin mobile starts to spin. The tuxedoed birds lifting and lowering at the ends of their strings.

Penguins playing! Oh so so silly!
Slide into water oh so chilly!

The recorded song is so saccharine and badly sung by a kid with a lisp that Paige knows she'll never get it out of her head. Just like she'll never forget the strings that shake the penguins as if they're shivering from the cold when the kid sings *chilly!*

She backs toward the door. Not wanting to take her eyes off the doll. Her mind races with the possibilities of what it would do if she did.

"Paige?"

At the sound of the voice the mobile quiets, goes dark. The penguins still swaying like New Year's Eve partygoers.

"Davis?"

"Paige . . . please—"

fzzzzzzz

White noise. Coming from outside the nursery. The bathroom she'd already checked.

It's the most important part of any funny story, Paige works to tell herself. *You can't leave now. This is the punch line.*

23

The living room is unlived in.

This has always been the impression it's left on Lily. The tall bookshelves, Turkish rugs, leather chairs, the lamps barely bright enough to cast any light through their thick shades. The lounge at a stuffy men's club. Lily doesn't ever come here to sit, but she likes the way it looks. She's always been a sucker for wanting to be invited into groups if only so she could turn them down. This room is like her own clubhouse. Formal, exclusive, memberless.

It's empty now too. No indication anyone has been in here for weeks.

She's not sure why but she tries her phone again. Calls Davis's number. This time it connects. A moment later there's the dull vibration of a phone receiving her call somewhere in the room.

It must be because she's making the call both from and to phones within the house that prevents the system from blocking it. That's what she guesses. There must be a reason, because it's not her imagination. The vibration she can feel like a beetle crawling up her leg.

She drops to her knees. Crawls over the rug, following the signal by touch more than the sound it makes.

It's there. Under the sofa. The aqua light of a phone's screen lit up by an incoming call.

Lily has to lie on her side to reach under and pull it out. In the second before the screen goes dark again she sees the photo Davis had up on his home screen. The two of them in wool sweaters and jeans rolled up to the ankles, holding each other on a bare stretch of Atlantic beach. Davis bending over to clench Lily in a kiss.

She's looking at the phone, considering calling Davis's number again if only to see the image of them together, when the blue square blinks to life on the inside of the right lens of her glasses. It wasn't working before—she'd tried using it to connect to her laptop, but nothing happened—and now it's active without her having anything to do with it.

It takes a moment to realize that the tiny square isn't a secondary monitor of her laptop screen. It's a mirror. One that looks up and behind where she is now, the details of the frame coming into focus piece by piece.

The robot looms over her prone body. The hammer handle still jammed down its throat, its skull cracked and oozing. Balancing on its waist and spasming in what must be an effort to keep its balance but appearing to Lily as a pantomime of vigorous self-pleasuring.

It can't be there, because it's dead. Destroyed.

It's there.

She pulls the glasses off and throws them across the room before she rolls onto her back, her fingers clenched into claws.

24

Paige enters the bathroom sideways. It feels safer somehow, leaving less of her exposed to direct attack. But then she catches herself in the mirror over the sink and sees how ridiculous she looks, sidling over the tiled floor like a halftime-show backup dancer.

The staticky white noise that drew her in here isn't a radio or speaker feedback. It's both sink taps on full.

Nobody's been in here since she passed through, unless Henry turned back while she was in the nursery to wash his hands and left the water on. Unlikely. He doesn't strike her as the type to leave messes behind. Which means someone else was here.

"Taps off," she says, and the last of the water swirls down the drain.

She quietly sings an altered version of the jingle from an old commercial. *Tap on, tap off. The tapper!* It makes her feel a little better. Jokes always do. Her own, anyway.

The bathroom is as empty as it was moments ago. There's no need to solve the mystery of the taps while standing here with the nervous tingling marching up her legs, so she moves toward the door again.

Scratching.

Barely audible, but she definitely hears it. Weak as a mouse building a nest between the walls. Except it isn't a mouse. And it's coming from inside the shower stall.

"Hello?"

For the second time in the same minute she feels ridiculous. *Hello?* As if an invisible serial killer hiding in here is going to introduce himself so long as she addresses him politely.

She slides to the shower stall and opens its broad, frosted glass door. Heavy and solid. You can feel how pricey it is, custom made, difficult to find. Lily-grade material.

The scratching comes and goes, but it's a little louder inside the stall. She steps onto its dry floor of poured concrete—an industrial touch to offset the modernist taps, the control screen set next to the silver tap handles. It's coming from the drain. Fingernails picking at the exterior of the pipe far below.

Paige gets on her knees.

"Hello?" she calls down the pipe. "Davis? Are you—"

The shower door slams shut.

There's nobody on the other side. The door has closed on its own, mechanized the same as the windows, the steel blinds, the taps.

Paige gets to her feet, noticing for the first time that there's no open space between the glass walls of the shower and the ceiling. Nowhere for her to even consider climbing out. Nowhere for her voice to escape.

She slaps against the door with her palm. Even from inside she can barely hear it.

"Help!"

The withheld desperation in her voice frightens her more than the door closing on its own. But she's been heard by something. The robot dog trots into the room and sits on the other side of the door, looking in at her, its head cocked.

The shower turns on.

It's one of those large, square showerheads positioned directly overhead that releases water in a simulation of rainfall. Cold, driving rain, in this case. There's not enough room in the corners of the stall to hide from it. Paige is instantly drenched and shivering.

"Hey there, buddy," she says to the dog. "Go get Lily."

The robot doesn't move.

"What about Henry?" Its ears pop up. "Okay, great. Go get Henry!"

The dog rises to all four legs, tail wagging. Turns and starts for the door. Just before it slips out, it abruptly stops. The tail comes down. Seemingly listening to a voice Paige can't hear.

"Go on!"

The dog doesn't hear her. It spins around and returns to the other side of the shower door and sits again, watching her. Behind the robot, the bathroom door slides closed.

"Shit," Paige says.

bleep

The shower's control screen blinks to life. The display taken up with the maximized, glowing digits of the water's temperature. Paige feels it warming only after seeing the number rising.

62 64 69

"No."

A single, ignored denial. Perhaps not ignored—it seems to provoke a spike in the water's temperature. The numbers leaping higher.

82 86 94 102

It's hard to see now.

The steam tumbles up from the floor in defiance of gravity, building a second wall against the glass. So hot it burns her throat to take it in. Waving it away only draws it against her, heavy and scalding as a horse blanket boiled in a pot. She tries to hold her breath but her body demands otherwise and she gasps in a fist of heat.

124 142 154 166 178

Paige attempts to scream but there's nothing to come out other than a choking squeak.

Her terror arrives as a separate matter from panic, at once expanding her senses—the heat, the blindness, the scorching movement of blood inside her—and narrowing her thoughts. A flickering of lived experiences passing through a pinhole. The snow clinging to the pines after a blizzard on her walk to kindergarten. Her lover in college sneaking out her dorm window wearing Scooby-Doo slippers. The single occasion that her father, droolingly drunk, told her he was proud of her.

186 198 208 214

She fights to keep standing. This is important for some reason she can't grasp. The pinhole of remembered things seals shut. She lurches and quarter-spins but stays on her feet as she's boiled alive.

On the other side of the door, the dog remains. Watching.

When the steam is a solid mass within the glass Paige finally yields, bumping against the door and sliding onto the shower's floor. Her legs and arms jerking, electrified, but she's well past consciousness. Muscle reflexes carrying out their final commands. The last one tells her hand to press against the door as if in farewell.

220

The water turns off.

The door opens an inch. The dog stands, tail looping in wild circles like a lasso. A human whimper of excitement escapes its widening jaws.

25

William isn't there. There's nobody behind her. For several seconds Lily claws at the air as if clearing it of any attacker that might materialize.

She *knows* what she saw in her glasses. The robot, threatening her, trying to frighten her. *C'mon, Lily*, she scolds herself. *That's not it. The robot wasn't there. Think it through.* So what was it really? What mistake of perception did she make to bring it into false being?

A connection error between her glasses and laptop? An optical illusion combining the dead screen and her own imagination?

William was *there*. That's the problem. Not as a reflection or software burp or anxious hallucination. It had been as real a presence as anything could be short of it touching her or striking her.

Which was what it had wanted to do. She'd felt it as certainly as she'd seen it coming at her.

She sits up at the waist and turns her attention to Davis's phone. She tries but can't make external calls on his phone either. Useless as it is, it does tell Lily some things nonetheless.

Davis was inside the house while Paige bandaged her wrist. The living room, specifically. Here. Or can she be entirely sure of that? His phone was under the sofa. It may be that Davis tossed it under there himself. It may be that someone else did.

The possible meanings of the phone bombard her thoughts, making her question whether it means anything at all. She wishes she could call Davis and ask where he is. This desire is followed by an urge she hasn't felt in weeks. She wishes she could call her mother.

Lily pockets the phone and debates whether she should confront Henry with it. Her decision depends on what she suspects is happening in the house—has already happened—and once she starts wondering about this, her mind creeps out of her control again. There's also her attachment to secrecy. Her and Davis. Her nature is to hold on to things even when there isn't a clear advantage to do so.

She'll keep the phone for now. Keep the questions she wants to ask Henry to herself. One clear memory comes through to her from an elective course in law she took in college. In cross-examination, a good attorney never asks a question unless she knows the answer in advance.

She decides to find Paige. Maybe she'll ask her about the phone. Maybe she'll keep it from her too.

In the main hallway, rounding the banister at the bottom of the stairs, she nearly runs into the dog coming down from the second floor, its plastic nails clipping on the wood.

MASON COILE

"Hey, you," she says.

The dog pauses at her feet. Its eyes goggle around in its head—*whirr-whirr*—as if its vision is blurry and it's trying to focus. *Click.* The eyes find her. Staring. She figures it's letting her pass and she's about to head upstairs when she notices water dripping onto the floor from the patchy hair of its muzzle.

She pauses. The dog doesn't drink, unless Henry has somehow figured out how to add that feature, to, what, make the simulation more realistic? Why would he bother? She bends to make sure, touching her hand to the warm drips. When she rises again her head is spinning.

Lily wobbles, slow but unstoppable. She's going to faint and wonders uselessly if there's a way to cut this failure off at the pass, and even this consideration drains the blood from her head and she begins to collapse.

Henry is there.

Coming down the stairs two steps at a time. He cups her head with an outstretched hand and prevents it from knocking against the banister's post as she goes down.

She tries to stand on her own, but her head is a balloon tethered to the rest of her by an unraveling length of ribbon. There's no choice but to yield to Henry, who lifts her up, carries her into the living room. Settles her into a leather armchair the size of a compact car.

"Where are your glasses?"

"What?"

"Your glasses—"

"I put them down somewhere. It doesn't—"

"Let me get you some water," he says, but her hand touches his arm and he stays. It may have only been accidental contact, but Henry chooses to see it as the desire to keep him close.

"Where's Paige?" she says.

"I'm not sure. I passed her in the hall upstairs a few minutes ago."

"We have to find her. Both of them."

"We will. But first we need to figure a way to get you out. That's the priority." He touches the same hand that had brushed his. "You and the baby—you're the priority."

Lily nods. He thinks it's in appreciation for his clarity of thought, but it's only her returning to her own considerations, keeping rhythm to her mental list-making with a bobbing chin. It doesn't lead her anywhere. Her chin puckers in a way he usually finds adorable but not now. Now it's from her trying not to cry.

"This can't be happening," she says. She places both of her hands over her belly. "It can't."

"There's an answer to this."

"Yeah? Doesn't feel like it."

"It does to me. And I'm going to find it."

"Even if we find a way out, you know you can't come with me," she says.

"Maybe I can. So long as we're together—maybe I can."

Lily touches Henry's cheek with the tip of her longest finger. The barest meeting of her skin to his. Yet it opens a door inside his chest and releases a bloom of heat that fills him with the idea that everything can be fixed, even the things there is no way out of. *There is a way.* He hears this and believes it before realizing it's William's voice in his head. Henry closes his eyes to prevent himself from shuddering.

Lily keeps her hand on his face and struggles to draw her gaze from where she found Davis's cell phone under the sofa. She hopes that her touch prevents Henry from following her line of sight. Has he already noticed it? It takes a determined effort, shifting in the chair, to pull them both away from the shadowed space.

"Henry?"

He opens his eyes. Lily has withdrawn her hand and he wills it to return, imagines it coming back to cup the side of his face with a ferocity that drains him. Hard wishing. Maybe he's not good at this. Or maybe there's no such thing as being good at wishing.

"We need a plan," she says.

26

Once the strength has returned to Lily's legs, Henry leads her to a small storage space under the stairs. Barely larger than a closet, the ceiling six feet high on the left but diagonally lowering to four feet on the right. There's nothing in there but a metal utility door in the wall.

"The circuit board," Henry announces with unintended formality.

"I don't think the problem is a blown fuse."

"We don't even *have* fuses. We're going to shut the house down. The power from here"—he knocks on the metal door—"and the computer system from the mainframe in the main bedroom."

Lily brightens. "Do it at the same time and the system will reboot to original settings."

"It should, yes."

She nudges Henry aside. "I've got this. You take the main-frame."

"It has to happen simultaneously."

She pulls out her phone. Checks the time. "We shut them down at exactly the top of the hour."

"Ten seconds of blackout should do it—"

"Then pull them both up."

Despite the events that have brought them to this point—he's already halfway to thinking of Davis's murder as just that, an "event," a perplexing phenomenon to be examined at a later time—Henry can't help but glow with delight at working together with Lily. They're a team again. Problem solvers. Engineers. Husband and wife.

* * *

Henry carries an ottoman from the living room to the storage space under the stairs for Lily to sit on. He pauses, wanting to deliver a kiss to her cheek, but decides the risk of her judging his timing to be off is too high, and he heads up to the second floor.

The mainframe unit is kept in the main bedroom closet. The room where Henry used to sleep until things eroded between them. He tries to tally the errors and miscommunications between then and now, the reasons behind his marital exile, but as always he can only come up with the sort of vague phrases you would use in an email with an acquaintance, or a divorce lawyer.

I was working too much.

She was emotionally adrift after selling her company.

We stopped being lovers and started being housemates.

None of them untrue. None of them sufficient.

He's about to venture into well-traveled speculations of exactly when the problems started—the turning point from a good marriage to a broken one—when he spots a lick of steam ushering out from under the closed bathroom door.

27

He walks blind into a wall of steam, the door sliding shut behind him.

The shower isn't on, but it must have been. And hot too. It's like moving through a huge, hot cloud.

It doesn't make sense. He didn't turn the shower on, and Lily was downstairs. Why would Paige do it? She must have, but he can't think of a good reason.

There is a way.

This time when he hears William's voice he's less sure it's in his head and not spoken by the robot's rubbery lips somewhere in the murk behind him. He tells himself there's no point in making sure because the machine he made can no longer move, the machine has never been anywhere outside the lab, the machine is dead.

He looks behind him anyway.

Nothing to see. But there's a sound. The shuddering squeak of skin drawn down over wet glass.

The shower stall. That's where it's coming from. He can hear that much.

He has his hands out in front of him, stepping through the maze of clouds, feeling for the glass. When they find it, his fingers slip over the patchy condensation, splaying out left and right, so that his face bumps into the transparent wall, his nose smarting at the impact. He rears back but leans in again a second later. Something is there. Inside the stall.

A shadow. A teetering stump. Looking like a monster out of a fairy tale. A goblin or troll.

Without intending to, Henry leans even closer to the glass. To confirm that he's wrong. Or if there is something there, to protect Lily from it.

A hand slaps against the inside of the glass.

The impact is fleshy and hard. The hand doesn't retreat but remains sucked to the glass as if letting Henry inspect it. Unmistakable cracks crisscrossing the sticky palms. The fingertips grubby with cheap paperback ink.

William's hand.

The robot rises up from the shower's floor. Grows taller on legs it never had when alive, the steady growth of a time-lapse weed. Henry can't see the features of his face other than the white tiles of his teeth, the lines shifting loosely in his mouth.

It stops growing once it stands at equal height to Henry.

The rubber hand tightens, the long nails set hard to the glass. They slide down the surface and send a dull shriek through the barrier. The first hand is joined by the second, also clawing against the glass. Faster now. The two hands rising and scratching. Digging through the wall.

Henry backs away from the shower. His breath taken in a series of gulps like a landed fish—*oh! oh! oh!*—that alarms him almost as much as the creature in the shower. He's careful with his steps, aware of the wet floor, the danger of slipping and falling and that thing finding a way out of the stall while he lies prone.

He keeps moving like this until he's in the hallway.

"Fan on," he says. "Close bathroom door."

The house computer follows both commands.

He'd like to carry on to the main bedroom and start the work of pretending what just happened didn't happen, but Lily's face appears in his mind. He has to be sure.

"Open bathroom door."

The fan has sucked away at least half of the steam from the room. It leaves the shower stall clearly visible, clearly empty. He's glad he doesn't have to step back inside to confirm it.

But there's something he can see now that he couldn't before.

A wet streak drawn over the bathroom floor, maybe a couple feet side to side. The width of a body. Starting from the shower door and curving toward the hall before fading to nothing.

28

Henry tries to decipher the streak as he would an unexpected glitch in a software model.

Where did that come from?

There is no one more adhered to reality than computer engineers. And yet he must concede that this is the question he found himself asking the most in his work when a phantom in the code threw things off.

His watch says 3:56. No time to ponder this any longer than he already has. Lily will be ready to shut the power off in a few minutes.

"Bathroom door close."

As it pulls shut, Henry averts his eyes from the narrowing gap just in case he glimpses the thing in the shower rising up again.

* * *

The main bedroom. Henry forces himself to keep thinking of it as this despite the fact that it's Lily's room now.

He opens the sliding closet doors to find a selection of his wife's dry-cleaned skirts and blouses neatly arranged on hangers and, softly sighing in the corner, the three-foot-tall mainframe unit that governs the operations of the house.

His checks his watch. 3:57.

Too much time to be crouched down like this waiting for the hour to turn, his knees already cranky about maintaining a baseball catcher pose.

He stands and goes to the bureau, where he's relieved to find that the framed photos of Lily and himself haven't been hidden away. This brings only momentary relief, as it's followed by the familiar observation that all the pictures are of Henry and Lily separately, never together. Each a solitary portrait.

Henry puts one hand on the side of his favorite photo of Lily (caught in a rare laugh), his other hand on a pic of himself (stern Henry, not quite following the joke). He slides the two frames closer until the enamel sides click together. As near to being a couple as he can make them.

But they're still not in the same shot. Still not touching. It's foolish how much this wounds him—how many times it's wounded him—but he's come to learn there are limits to how much reason can insulate you from hurt.

He returns to the closet and bends down in front of the mainframe. Rests his wrist atop his thigh. Pinches the red power switch on top of the unit between his fingers and watches the second hand.

"Three . . . two . . ."

* * *

". . . one . . ."

Lily flips the main power switch on the circuit board. The storage room blinks into darkness. She feels the entire house do the same, the darkness crashing through the halls and rising to the ceiling.

* * *

Henry pulls the red switch off on the mainframe. Its humming is silenced. It makes him think of an animal smothered in its sleep.

He starts to count to ten.

"One, two, three—"

* * *

"—four, five—"

As she counts, Lily hears something other than her voice. A weight dragging itself over the main hall floor. Coming closer.

It becomes more particular between each of the seconds. The hush of clothing passing over the varnished floorboards. The click of nails digging into the wood.

"—six, seven, eight—"

The weight is a body. The nails are attached to a false hand. The dragging required because the body has no legs.

"Who's there?" she says, but she knows.

The scraping is very close now, only inches from her feet. She can almost feel the touch of the rubber fingers and it makes her skin crawl.

"—nine, ten."

Lily turns on the main power switch. The lights return to life. She spins around.

29

Henry turns the mainframe back on. It starts up its long sigh and he can't help hearing it as a living thing—this time a human surgical patient coming out of anesthetic.

He starts for the main-bedroom door. Something stops him, something not quite right. It takes a second to realize that it's the pictures on the bureau.

The ones of Lily and himself that he slid together are now apart. He didn't do it. In fact, they're even farther apart than they were to begin with, so that each of them is past the edge of the bureau's top, teetering.

His hand snaps out and catches the portrait of Lily before it can fall, but the photo of himself tumbles over the edge. Smashes on the wood floor.

He gets down on his knees. Picks up the larger pieces of glass and tosses them into the wicker wastebasket. He asks himself how

MASON COILE

this could have happened but, having no answer, concentrates on finding each of the shards, from biggest to smallest. Lily often pads around the house in bare feet. And if you don't get the little pieces they can sometimes stay there for months, awaiting a victim. Long enough for a baby to grow into a crawler. He imagines a chip of glass finding a chubby knee or hand and bends lower, scouring.

Henry's hand discovers patches of wetness in the carpet. He leans down to sniff it, but it has no smell.

The robot dog thumps into the room. Its muzzle isn't dripping water anymore, but the patchy hair there is still wet-darkened.

"You," Henry says. "What did you spill?"

The dog's tail rotates faster and faster as if attempting liftoff from its back end. It wants to show Henry something. If he would just bend down he'd see it. The dog whines, pleading. It so badly wants to show him the body under the bed.

Paige's eyes peer out from the shadows, glassy and white as a pair of shellacked eggs. Her features fixed in an expression of astonishment. Her skin red and flaking with burns, not that she feels them.

The dog whines at a higher pitch, insistent that Henry look under the bed, but he doesn't.

"Go on. Get out," Henry says.

The dog stays where it is. Its tail held up as if a finger requesting clarification.

"Go!"

The tail lowers and the dog trots out. It leaves Henry alone in the room, though he doesn't feel that way.

30

Lily paces around in a tight circle in the front hall. When she'd turned the power on, she looked quickly behind her from the storage space under the stairs and found nothing there. Yet there had been. An oily trace of its scent. A heaviness, an intrusion that had spoiled the air somehow, leaving it difficult to breathe, like driving past an abattoir with the windows down.

She hears Henry coming down the stairs but won't let herself look up at him. The last thing she needs is for him to see how shaken she is, though she can't figure out why hiding this is so important to her.

"What happened?" He stops on the bottom step. "Lily? You look—"

"Did you hear anything? When you were upstairs?"

He considers telling her about the pictures but decides against it. Lily has even less patience for the mystical than he does, so the idea that an unseen hand pushed their portraits from the top of the bureau would only irritate her.

"No," he says. "Why?"

"I thought I did."

"What was it?"

"I thought—" She pulls herself back with a self-directed scoff. "Nothing. It was nothing."

Lily starts typing on the keyboard in the wall next to the front door. He can see her shoulders trembling.

"Did it work?"

She keeps typing as if she hadn't heard him.

"Lily? Did it—"

"No." She turns to face him. "It didn't."

Henry comes all the way down to the main floor. Places his hands atop her shoulders, hoping this contact will settle them. Instead, the muscles twitch and jump all the more against his touch.

"We're going to crack this," he says, lifting his hands away.

"Because we're smarter than everyone else?"

"Yes. Well, *you* are, anyway."

Lily turns and meets his eyes directly for a short moment before focusing on a point below them instead, as if holding silent communications with his chin. She manages a partial smile. It's little more than a reflex of politeness, the least she can do. Yet he allows himself to see it as a first step toward a more full reconciliation, as if she'd raised herself onto her toes to deliver a kiss.

"Why did you do it?" she says.

He's speechless. How does she know? It doesn't matter. She knows what he did, and it's over. His life, his freedom. Far worse, his marriage. He's finished and even as he gives up trying to come up with a lie there's no part of the truth he can translate into even the simplest words.

"Why make William?" Lily says.

It's all he can do to conceal the relief from his expression. The best thing to do is not wait, not let her take him in with her evaluating gaze. Answer her question.

God knows he's asked the same of himself many times. Along with the other questions that followed it. Why risk your happiness for a shoddy toy? Why do it alone? Lily already understands what it is to lose yourself in work, so he needn't point out the thrill of seeing an idea come into being, of surpassing your own expectations. But why start in the first place when you had everything you wanted? Lily, the house, the baby on the way. The truth is he knows the answer. There's no way Henry could share it without hurting Lily's feelings. But the fact is, he was lonely.

"I'm not sure," he says.

"It's just strange how one day you're not making a robot, and the next day you've got a list of things you want me to order so you can make a robot, and the day after that, all you're doing for every spare moment of the day is making that robot."

"I regret that."

"No, you don't."

"He wasn't worth what he cost me."

"William might not have turned out the way you thought it would, I get that. But it makes it no less impressive an accomplishment."

She means it. Lily can forgive pretty much any sacrifice made in the name of a successful experiment. Her own business ventures prove it. She pours all of herself into making something new, the money people swoop in and buy it, and she's out. Which is fine with her. She's told Henry multiple times that she's not interested in running things, only starting things. What those things go on to become—whether they solve existing problems or create new ones—is of next to no interest to her. She says this is evidence of her entrepreneurial spirit. Henry recognizes it as a more comfortable way of describing pure ambition.

"I've mentioned my math teacher in high school before, right?" he says.

"Your first mentor."

"It's funny but the whole time I was working on William she was watching over me. I felt her there. My parents too, sometimes. All of them dead now, but they were up in that lab with me, pushing me on."

"I know what you mean," she says. "You wanted to make them proud."

"And it sort of worked for a while. But once William—once he became who he was—I didn't feel them with me anymore."

She takes a step back from him to get a better read of his face. It's her Lily move, and it never fails to take him by surprise: the abrupt turn from conversation to evaluation.

"Why not?" she says.

"I think they saw it before I did."

"The problem."

"Yes. They saw there was a problem with William."

"That wasn't your fault."

"I tried to tell myself that too. I'm not sure I'll ever be convinced of it."

"How could you have known?" She crosses her arms. "You made a program. The program mutated in an unanticipated way. It happens a lot with AI."

"You're talking about hidden biases that get smuggled into software. Prejudices left behind like fingerprints."

"Sure. Not that I blame coders for that either. It's next to impossible to keep the programming process perfectly sterilized."

"But that's the thing. I'm not talking about William's program."

Lily pauses a second, and he feels her taking him in at a new level of seriousness. "What are you talking about, then?"

"When you create a new life—a robot, a program, a baby— you're not just making a being, you're making a *space*. An absence inside the presence. Kind of like building a ship and launching it out to sea but without anything stored in the hold."

"So William put something rotten inside itself? That's what you're saying?"

"I think something came along and decided to take up the space inside him."

Henry shakes his head, an offer to drop this topic here and now. He's gone further than he intended and his thoughts are undeveloped—he'd barely had them at all before this moment— and it's never wise to discuss complex ideas with Lily before having them worked out. But she widens her eyes, inviting him to go on.

"I was wrong to assume that giving William intelligence and a body and a mind would define the boundary of what he was," Henry says. "He was unique. And in his uniqueness, he sent out a beacon to other influences, other presences. Why not? He was interesting to me. Maybe he was interesting to them too."

"So there was a digital parasite attached to it? Something that came in the parts I ordered for you? Are you saying it was hacked?"

"Not in the sense you mean."

"What sense do you mean?"

He wipes a hand down the side of his face to give himself time to decide whether to say what's in his head or keep it to himself. It turns out not to require a decision at all, because the next thing he knows he's saying it.

"Maybe I was lazy in programming ethical parameters. Maybe I gave him too much independence and he went down the wrong path. But there was something bad in him—there *came to be* something bad in him—that wasn't precisely me, and wasn't precisely him either. Something found an opportunity in him."

"It almost sounds like you're—"

Now it's Lily's turn to shake her head to avoid carrying her thought further.

Henry is going to ask about it, see if she's letting the possibilities flow in the same direction he's already headed in, when he's stopped by the music. Muffled bass licks, followed by guitar power chords. Coming from upstairs.

Lily instantly starts up the stairs after it.

"I don't think you should go—"

But she's not listening to him.

31

He can't stop her by force. And he can't order her to stay with him. This is Lily, after all. Even if she has betrayed her vows to him and now, trapped in this house with her husband, she is still more concerned about finding her lover than making corrections—Henry believes he has no right to tell her what to do.

So he does what's acceptable. He gives her a few seconds' head start before following her up the stairs.

Lily is moving faster than he guessed she was able. When he reaches the top of the stairs she's already taking her first step to the attic lab.

The music is louder up here. The bass moving like an animal

through the walls. Henry isn't a hard rock fan—he wouldn't say he's much of a music expert in any genre—but he knows the song. AC/DC's "Back in Black."

Lily is going to where the music is coming from. Where William's body is. The thought of her being in the same room with its mustard-bloodied corpse troubles him more than he could explain. She shouldn't go up there alone.

A squeak. Followed by a repetition of squeaks, coming from behind him.

Henry spins around.

The little magician. Not there when he made it past the top of the stairs a second ago and now pedaling around and around the same spot in a delirious circle. Henry didn't know it could do that. He didn't know it could go that fast.

"What are you doing?" he asks, more to himself than the toy.

The little magician pedals in tightening circles without reducing its speed, like a dog chasing its own tail. The circles drift closer to the edge of the top stair so that it will fall if it doesn't stop. Henry thinks of bending down and stopping it, but he doesn't want to touch the thing, his own creation now transformed into something unwholesome and bizarre.

The bicycle's front wheel spins over the edge. The magician's hat ducks down. Then it's out of sight, a thick clanking down each step like a tambourine smacked by a boxing glove.

There's little point in watching its fall, but it seems that's what it wants from Henry.

He has the tingling sensation at the back of his head that is the initial, unconscious alert that you may be about to step into a trap.

It doesn't stop him. He takes a step toward the edge of the stairs to look down at the tumbling magician's progress.

* * *

The door to the lab has been left open. Lily nudges it wider. As soon as she takes a step inside, the music stops.

She glances over her shoulder expecting to find Henry behind her, but he isn't there. He'd been following her up the stairs only seconds earlier—she heard him coming, though she refused to turn around for fear of him seeing it as her needing him—and now she finds herself wishing he were there.

There's a click from somewhere inside the lab. Followed by a wash of static.

She has to be brave for Davis.

She needs to find Davis.

Lily cycles these thoughts in a loop, reminding herself so her legs keep moving through the tightly assembled tables, her feet stepping on the clear squares between the snaking power cords. She takes extra care to not let any part of her touch the disassembled arms or legs or cut pieces of plastic skin piled to the table edges. She also makes a point of not letting her eyes rest on the destroyed robot on the floor.

William's radio. Still on the table in the position where the robot had left it. This is the source of the white noise and, she guesses, the music from moments ago. Its circular tuner window glowing underwater green.

Lily picks it up, turns it over in her hand as if inspecting it for strings or some other trickery. She doesn't like touching the same surface that the robot had not too long ago, imagining a trace of the humid grease his non-skin left behind.

As soon as she moves to put the radio down, the tuner needle moves.

Lily tosses it away from her.

But it doesn't turn off. She watches the needle continue to slide over the numbers under the green dial. Not a shift to a particular station, but a smooth and continuous rotation through the entire range of frequencies, round and round.

As it moves, the static is interrupted by jolts of music and voices—single-word declarations of news announcers, commercials, sports analysis.

Big. You. Town.

A used-car-lot man, a chirpy child, a woman doing Marilyn Monroe. Moods. Shards. Nonsense straining for meaning.

The needle continues to swim in a circle, but the radio's volume dwindles. The batteries on their last legs. Lily lifts the radio's speaker closer so she can hear. It disgusts her now as it had when she first touched it, but she intuits the necessity of understanding the random words.

The volume dims to almost nothing. She brings the radio closer. The instant it touches her skin the words assemble into a sentence.

The source of the voices continues to change—a lisping toddler, a bellowing preacher, a deathbed whisper—but selected by one mind.

So. Dark. Here.

Lily turns the radio off. This time she throws it away. A proper, full-armed pitch that sends the shell of its body leaping off the tabletop and over the floor until it rests against the far corner of the lab's wall. From this distance, it looks to her like something once alive but no longer. A poisoned sewer rat.

The rat's eye blinks open. Glows green.

"Fuck," Lily says, backing up.

The radio finds a new set of words and announces them at full blast. Not picked out of the stream of random singers or news readers this time, but spoken in William's voice.

I'll. Show. You.

32

The bicycle hits the marble floor of the foyer, and the impact sends the magician flying.

Henry watches the little rider spin off the seat, its arms waving up at him in a series of hellos and goodbyes. It spins on its back, knees stiffly bent, before settling an arm's length from the front door.

Is this what the robot toy wanted him to see? Its suicide? Why does he feel so certain that the magician intended to show him anything at all?

Henry is unsettled in a way he hadn't been a moment ago. He's also more curious. He creeps halfway down the stairs.

The robot dog comes into view, clicking its nails along the main-floor hall. It's wagging its tail and jumping up and down on its front paws in a way Henry has never seen it do before, as if playing a game with some unseen friend. He might have guessed it was a malfunction if it weren't for the dog's eyes. The only part of it that is still. More than that. The eyes are fixed on something in the main-floor hallway.

Henry takes another step down. Another. Far enough that he can lean over the railing and look down the hall to his right to see what the dog sees.

A body lurches into view.

It's wrapped in a clear plastic tarp, the inside folds smeared with blood. A man. He holds his arms out in front of him, feeling his way forward, the plastic crinkling and popping. Each step threatening to buckle his knees, but he doesn't fall.

Henry works to tally the pieces of reality laid out before him. It's the blood that makes it difficult. Coming from Davis's chest and finding its way to his feet. A puddle that leaps against the inside of the plastic with each of his strides.

He watches the man's progress in disbelief. In part because he'd seen what was done to him—what *he* did to him—on the surveillance video. But also because Davis's movements, the fact that he's standing and chucking his feet forward from inside a thick bag freshly streaked and smudged with blood, seem to defy physics as well as the law of death.

The robot dog moves in tight circles around the struggling Davis as if he were a new plaything. Its tongue stretched out to an obscene length, the tip of it finding spots of blood on the inside of the plastic and attempting to lick it off. Each time the tongue fails to connect with the warm fluid the dog whines in yearning.

It puzzles Henry. Even as he's reeling with astonishment and revulsion, he's also aware, on a quieter level, of the impossibility of what the dog is doing. Its software includes no sense of smell or taste. It experiences no hunger aside from its battery that requires recharging, and that isn't something it has knowledge of. Yet here it is, sniffing and licking, a keen appetite brought into being.

Davis is headed toward the front door. It's hard to imagine he could see anything through the distortions of the tarp, but he seems to be intent on getting there. Henry wonders if he should let him. Wonders if he'll have to stop him if he begins banging on the door or demanding to be let out.

But then Davis veers into the living room off the hall. An accident of misbalance that took the appearance of an abrupt change of mind. Within seconds he has shuffled out of Henry's view.

The dog starts after him.

"Stay," Henry says.

The dog sits.

Henry hurries down the stairs, rifling through the first questions that come to him. How is Davis still alive? How did he get down here? Who did this to him? Henry knows nothing of what it takes to kill a man, so he shouldn't be shocked to find that a pair of scissors thrust into his chest isn't quite enough, at least not right away. Maybe Davis came down under his own steam, maybe he was carried. It must have happened when Henry was blacked out. Did he do this? All of it? Himself?

These thoughts thrum through his head before a new line of questions pounds against the inside of his skull.

Do you save this man? Do you hide him? Do you finish him?

"Let me help you," Henry says.

He's made it to the foyer so that he's close enough to speak at a level he hopes won't reach up two floors to be detected by Lily. Measured, level, kind. Yet when Davis hears Henry, he cowers in terror without turning to confirm who's there, so that he almost falls backward.

"It's alright. I'm sorry for what happened. But I can help you now."

Davis remains still. Perhaps he's deciding whether Henry is sincere, or perhaps he's trying to devise a means of counterattack for when Henry comes at him again.

"I won't hurt you."

This decides it. The assurance that Henry won't hurt him is taken by the man to mean its opposite, and he resumes leaping and reaching forward inside the tarp, pulling himself into the living room.

Henry is on the move. The man's terror is harder to witness than his injuries, and the thought that Henry is the cause of both threatens to empty his stomach onto the floor.

It's over, and it's good that it's over. He thought he'd murdered this man. But here he is, still alive. Will Lily forgive him? Likely not. But there is room for an honest explanation, and so long as that exists, there's room for understanding. The relief at not having to cover up the truth anymore settles his stomach like the first sip of wine at a gathering of strangers.

"I promise. I won't—"

Before Henry can reach Davis, the living room's heavy doors emerge from the slots built into the wall and slide shut.

Henry is left alone in the hallway. He is about to bang at the wood but switches back to thinking about Lily, keeping this from Lily, just in case. He doesn't shout Davis's name or knock. He doesn't do anything other than scan the hallway floor, checking to see if any of the blood found its way out.

33

Lily comes down from the attic lab contemplating—if she set the house on fire, could the firemen break their way in and save her before she burned to death? A radical plan. That's what Davis called her boldest initiatives. "Lily's always got the radical plan," he'd say after she explained doubling down on an experiment or playing fast and loose with regulators. There was admiration in it, but also wariness, the hinted reminder that not every gamble pays off.

As for the fire idea, it's a nonstarter anyway. She's terrified of being burned, for one thing. Smoke inhalation alone would be a huge risk to the baby. And then there's the question of whether firemen could get through the house's military-grade glass and metal blinds with axes and shovel handles. She guesses not.

Everything had to be the best for Lily, especially her gear, her tech, her labs. The security doors and blinds in her house. You had to be surrounded by good stuff to make good stuff happen, she thought. She wasn't sure where this belief had come from.

There was never any question about her being ambitious. Since high school it's been her "thing," which she's always regarded as a socially acceptable way of diminishing her accomplishments. The type of men who like her always say they find her drive sexy. She believes them. She finds it sexy too.

But the size and scope of her ambition and her vast yearning for success had no clear source. Her parents were mild and loving in an embarrassed, Minnesotan way. She liked money but didn't measure herself by it. Professional accolades were nice, but fame struck her as an unnecessary burden.

The real kick came from challenging and surpassing yourself. Starting out with a plan not because shareholders demanded one, but because *you* did. Lily's greatest projects were those initiated without foreknowledge of what they might become.

For Lily, that was what it truly meant to play God. It wasn't about making difficult ethical decisions, or setting down absolute rules, or building guardrails. God didn't do that. God created. If beauty or discovery was the result—if chaos was the result—it didn't matter. It only mattered that something astonishing was born.

That was why she asked Henry why he'd made William. She wondered if he felt the same way.

Lily's coming along the second-floor hallway when she hears the dull smack of the living room's door sliding into place. Did the house computer do that? Did Henry?

Another door clicks opens to her right as she passes it. The nursery.

It's as if the house wants her to go inside. Does that mean she should? The smart decision would likely be to resist such an obvious invitation. But she's already trapped. And the only way out is to follow every opening to its end.

* * *

Davis looks back and catches the living room door squeezing out the last inches of open space and then, with the solid clack of a shotgun pumping a shell into the chamber, it locks shut.

It's good that there's a barrier between himself and Henry. Henry did this to him. Hurt him. Wrapped him up in plastic like a frozen chop. At least he isn't in this room now. He wouldn't be able to think his way through his terror if he was. But the problem remains the same as it did since he regained consciousness: how to get out?

He doesn't have much time. He's still bleeding, the warm blood trickling under his clothes. He's still in shock.

He scans the room through the distortions of the tarp. There might be places he could hide here. No, no, *no*. He can't hide. He's injured, he needs medical attention, he's probably dying. He needs to *get out*.

As Davis shuffles forward he tries to summon the image of Lily's face to his mind as motivation, a reason to find a way out of this polished, mahogany-paneled horror house. Instead, it's his mother who comes to him. The woman, long dead, he's come to reflexively dismiss as a nonpresence in his past ("We were never close") is with him now, telling him to keep going, to keep thinking because he was always a smart boy.

The window. He's been heading toward it since the door closed, but only now does he notice why.

It's been opening on its own for the last few seconds. The enormous, heavy pane sliding upward, leaving a good-sized gap at the bottom of the six-foot-high frame. Room enough for a man to fit through.

Why is it opening now? He has no time to be curious about things like that. This is a chance. The only one he'll get. Once he escapes and waves down a car or bangs on a neighbor's door and gets to an emergency room, he can pull a sensible narrative together.

The window looks onto the broad side yard. Dusk has fallen outside. Through the pines that mark the property line, he can see the inflated ghosts and Frankenstein monster on the lawn next door.

Davis throws himself into the window's open gap, thinking that his body will tumble onto the ground and he can sort himself out from there. It half works. The tarp catches on the window ledge, and he stops short, his head outside and the rest of him still crinkling and kicking inside.

Another couple of solid pushes from his legs would get him over the edge, but he has nothing left. He used his last bit of strength to get here. He senses his bottom half struggling to gain traction, and he can hear the tarp folding around his movements like a snake wrapping tighter around him, waiting out the exhaustion of its prey.

Davis cranes his head around. Looks up. The window's frame is solid oak, wide as outstretched arms. The pane is still rising, bumping to a stop when it can go no farther.

There's a sound from the hallway on the other side of the sliding door. Is Lily there? Paige?

"Please," he attempts to say, but it comes out as a bubble of coppery spit that pops against the plastic that is pulled against his face with every breath.

He struggles to move the tarp away from his mouth. When he's done his best, he takes in as much air as he can, but it's sour inside the bag, hot and already recycled through his fevered lungs, and he coughs.

The sound seems to trigger another sound. A sharp creak, then a crack. Bright and neat as a partly sawed tree in the second it pops. Falls. Hard as splintered ice.

Davis looks up again, his vision cleared by sudden tears, to see the window coming down.

He jolts. Once. Feels it. The impact, the split spine. His head almost entirely severed from the rest of him. Hanging on by a belt of skin. He feels all of it.

His mother comes to him again. Not in his mind, but right there, standing in the side yard, the inflatable ghost and Frankenstein's monster waving through the branches behind her.

She's trying to tell him something. A statement of her position in relation to him. She's close, or coming closer, or she's too far, she's drifting away and he'll have to look for her in the place he's going—he can't figure out what it is. He wishes she would tell him how to find her. He wishes he had a sliver more time to remember her name, so he could say it, feel it one last time on his tongue, but he—

34

Lily approaches the crib as if it were a sleeping lion.

Soft, dancer's steps. Arms held out at her sides. One foot carefully finding the center of the train track's oval on the floor. Her next step puts her on the other side and she slowly raises her foot again before stepping forward to make sure it doesn't accidentally catch on the dining car or the diesel engine at the front.

The stuffed giraffe and hippo are propped against the slats of the crib, but a blanket covers a lump in its middle. Lily chokes down a ball of sourness that rises up her throat, reaches in, and pulls the blanket back.

It's not immediately clear what she's looking at. The items themselves are normal, familiar, but their arrangement is perverse. The doll. The handheld baby monitor. The latter tucked under the hem of the doll's dress.

Something did that. This occurs to Lily first. A thought followed by an even more troubling one. *It wanted me to find it.*

Lily would like to leave but she's unable to move.

The doll's dress glows green. The baby monitor screen has come to life.

It wants to show me something.

Lily bends over the side of the crib so she can pull the monitor out. She tries not to touch any part of the doll. The process is weirdly invasive, surgical.

When it's in her hand she looks down at the screen and sees the view from the camera located in the corner of the nursery's ceiling. There's Lily. The feed a quarter second delayed from the movements she makes and their representation on the monitor.

She looks at the camera. As soon as she does, it moves. Shifts the aim of its lens from the crib to the opposite corner of the room. A spot behind Lily.

Lily turns to follow where the camera is pointing. Nothing there.

The lights dim, then turn off completely, casting the room into darkness except for the glow from the baby monitor. She looks back down at it. The night-vision capability is on.

She can hear the camera moving, focusing on the far corner. It finds something there now. She almost swallows her tongue holding back a scream.

William.

Skin-ripped, skull-caved. Standing lopsided on legs he has grown or stitched on or imagined into being. His baggy, formal suit stained with the thick mustard-blood that hangs in a lengthening string from the corner of his mouth.

Lily points the monitor at the corner, using the glow from the screen to illuminate the space. It's just an empty corner of the room.

She looks back at the monitor. William is still there. Except now he's closer to the crib. To her.

Lily flashes the light into the corner again. Empty. She closes her eyes to keep from looking at the screen, but the darkness is frightening in a different way. She opens them.

William is standing next to her.

The toy train starts up. She hears it chittering around the oval of the track behind her. She throws the baby monitor to the floor. Her breath squeezes in her throat as if through a juice box straw.

Lily backs away from the crib. The train is speeding its rotation. Faster and faster until the engine leaps from the track, the cars clattering onto their sides behind it.

Her heel snags on the derailed train and she falls back, arms circling as if attempting to swim up to the surface after some unseen thing grabbed her by the leg.

She lands onto her back, rolls to her side, her cheek against the floor. Staring directly at the baby monitor she'd tossed, now only inches from her face.

The screen is off. She reaches out to push it away, but she's not fast enough. The monitor flashes green. William is kneeling over her, reaching to stroke her hair. Take her by the throat. His long-fingered hand reaching to touch her pregnant belly.

Lily kicks against the floor, sliding backward, her fingernails clawing at her sides. She chokes back another stifled scream and keeps going until she's across the nursery's threshold and into the hallway. Without letting herself look into the room she reaches up, finds the handle, and heaves the door closed.

35

Henry hears two slams, one after the other.

He's pretty sure one comes from the second-floor hallway. The other is the window in the living room. On the other side of the locked sliding door. He can tell from the sound of the sill, something cracking under force, like a tree branch or a length of two-by-four or bones.

It leaves him motionless in the front foyer, thinking not about the sounds but what it would mean to be honest with Lily.

He's a terrible liar. He's always thought this about himself, and Lily's often said it too. But now he thinks it may be more accurate to say that he's never attempted lying before. Never had to, so it was assumed within his marriage that it was a skill he didn't have. Yet he hasn't told Lily what he saw on the surveillance video, what he must have done to the man in the living room. Lies of omission, perhaps, but there they are, successful. He doesn't know why he did it. He doesn't remember doing it. But maybe this is the way for most killers: a blackout of rage that enables the doing of terrible things.

He can't dwell on those parts. The guilt. The getting away with it or not. The prospect of being arrested, tried, imprisoned. It's essential that all those issues be bound up and locked into a vault for the time being.

He has to think about Lily.

And in thinking about Lily, he has to maintain the deception that he has no idea what happened to Davis, or where he is now. Either Davis got out and will send help that will arrive within minutes, or he didn't, and it's just Henry and Lily sealed inside the house. And Paige. Where is Paige? Either way, telling Lily the truth won't change anything of importance.

Even as Henry rationalizes his lying, he's aware of the truth that lives beneath it. He's doing all of this in the hope that he can find a way back to her. The man in the tarp will disappear. The surveillance video will never be seen. Everything else that's happening will be a strange story shared between the two of them. The first step on the path to reconciliation.

He's not sure how it will work. But keeping his focus on Lily, leaving a space for her, is the only way he can move forward. And telling her he murdered the man she had feelings for isn't going to help.

Now that he's really trying, Henry acknowledges that perhaps he isn't such a terrible liar at all.

* * *

He comes up onto the second floor and spots his wife on her back outside the nursery door.

"Lily?"

She doesn't make any sign that she hears him outside of taking in a shuddering breath.

"What happened?"

"He was in there," she says.

"Who?"

"You know fucking who."

Henry goes to her. At his approach she slides her back against the far wall across from the nursery door.

"Are you hurt?"

"I'm—" She puts her hands on her belly. Feels the top of it, under it. Searching for movement. A heartbeat. A kick from inside. "I'm okay."

The two of them listen to the house. That's what they try to tell themselves, that it's the house doing these things. But that is just the shock talking. Because it isn't the house that has become unpredictable, hostile, alive. It's the presence moving through it.

Henry crouches next to her and puts his arm around her shoulders. He's surprised that she lets him. It's not necessarily a show of tenderness, though he shapes it into this in his thoughts.

"What is he thinking?" She looks at him. "What does he want?"

"You mean William," he says.

"Yes."

"But he's—"

"Just tell me, Henry."

He hadn't asked himself this before, not in the terms Lily has framed. So he offers her his best answer as it comes to him.

"His thoughts are . . . wrong."

"A programming error."

"No, something else. Something foreign."

"Okay, okay," Lily says, choosing her next question among the swirling options. "What does this foreign presence want?"

"The same thing as William. To do things. So it can feel things."

"Does that include killing us?"

"I think it could. Yes."

"That's his endgame," she says. "Seeing us dead?"

"That's probably just a bonus."

"So what's the real win?"

"Getting out of this house."

"Guess we have that in common."

Lily stuns Henry with a laugh, high and ringing, a second-glass-of-wine sound. Henry mistakes it for warmth, the two of them joined together in dark humor aimed at an antagonist to both of their interests. He decides to venture a thought meant to bring them closer still.

"Gotta admit, it's a hell of a puzzle."

Lily's humor instantly falls away. "What is?"

"William. I mean, he's dead—and yet, he's not."

Lily eyes him like a stranger on the subway whose hand had been drifting close to snatch her purse.

"Earlier, when you were talking about absences inside the

presence—about something bad finding its way into William—I thought you were talking about a devil," she says. "Now it sounds like you're saying he's a ghost. He can't be both."

"Why not?"

"Because the distinction is more than just different versions of being dead."

"And AI is more than a different version of being alive."

She blinks. "Help me with that."

"It's not only novel technology. It's human-created life that isn't human. A first."

"So?"

"So we only have the most elementary notions about the philosophical and moral implications they bring. But the *spiritual* aspect? We haven't even bothered to raise the question."

She blinks again and has to bring a finger to rub her eyelids to stop them from blinking. "How is any of this *helpful*, Henry?"

"I don't know that it is. But I do know that whatever distinctions we hold between ghosts and demons, any of that stuff—none of it is likely to be reproduced the same way in AI. It will all be new."

Lily is following what he's saying and she doesn't like it. When her mind is opened to unpleasant possibilities, she defends herself by reasserting their impossibility. A self-contradicting circle. Not that Henry has ever dared to call it that out loud.

"So that talking mannequin of yours has a soul?" she says, her voice rising, shifting from impatience and blooming into anger. "Is that where you're going? That . . . thing, that oversized doll you'd use to scare kids on Halloween is *haunting* us?"

"Consciousness. Ideas. Desires. If he has all those things—and if humans can retain a presence on this side after we die *because* of those same things—why not him?"

Lily gets to her feet faster than he thought she could.

"Because he's not human, Henry!" She's shouting now, walking toward the stairs down to the first floor. "He's fucking nothing!"

"Lily, wait," Henry says.

She doesn't look at him. But she pauses, ready to evaluate what he's about to say.

"I have an idea."

36

Henry searches through the spare parts, rubber limbs, and power cords strewn over the tables and floor of his lab. From the open doorway, Lily keeps watch. Not on Henry, but on William's lifeless stump of a body, still slumped on the floor, its mouth stretched wide and the yellow gunk of its insides drying down the length of its throat like some hideous, moldy garden fountain.

"What are you looking for?"

"Something long," he says without looking back at her. "Something that can stand straight but also bend a little bit to go around—"

"Henry?"

"Yeah?"

"Can I ask you to do something for me?"

He straightens and squints back at her. "Sure."

"Can you make sure that thing is dead?"

He goes through a mini pantomime of pretending not to know what she means at first, then looking down at William, shrugging— *If it makes you happy*—and then taking a position over him.

From where he stands, Henry can see down the robot's throat. There's no tube of flesh leading to a stomach, no simulated organs of any kind. It's just an opening. Within is a tangle of wires and metal pieces, all crusted in the yellow fluid. A bag of garbage. It's hard to believe it was able to move at the beginning of the day. This hobby of Henry's, cobbled together from thirdhand online dealers. An hour ago it could think and read and hurt and lie.

Henry kicks the robot in the chest. It topples onto its side, rolling back and forth for a moment, as if in an attempt to right itself. And then it lies still.

He doesn't check to see if Lily is satisfied by this, just goes straight back to looking through the items on the tables.

"This'll do it," he says.

Henry lifts up a coil of thick industrial cord and shows it to Lily.

"A power cord," she says.

"A flagpole," he says.

* * *

Lily is already on the landing outside the lab, waiting for Henry to join her. He drags the cord behind him, and once he's out he tells the door to close.

"What are we working on here, Henry?"

"It's basically an SOS signal."

"How's that?"

"We attach a T-shirt to the top of this thing and write a message on it—"

"Like 'Help!'"

"Yeah, 'Help!' would work."

"Great. So how's anybody going to see it?"

"We feed the cord up the chimney through the spare-room fireplace."

"It's gas."

"Gas. Wood. It still has a hole in the top. And if we can push our flag out of it someone will see it eventually."

Henry pulls the padlock out of his pocket, loops it through the latch, snaps it shut. Lily watches him.

"Why is the only analog lock in this entire house on the outside of your lab door?" she says. "To keep me out?"

"Maybe at first."

"And then it became a habit."

"No. Then I think I did it to keep him in."

"You thought he might've escaped if you didn't have it there?"

"I guess I thought he might think of a way."

"He's dead now," she says. "We just proved it. Why are you locking it now?"

"Same reason," Henry says.

Lily holds out her hand. "My turn," she says.

Henry gives her the key.

"Now let's fly our freak flag," she says.

37

Henry's on his hands and knees in front of the fireplace in the spare room where he's been sleeping. He's got his hand partway up the flue, feeding the stiff cord higher.

Lily leans over his shoulder. "Is it working?"

"It's tricky. I think I'm almost there, but—"

"But what?"

"You've got to waggle it around at the top to find the way through and my hand can't get high enough."

Lily is immediately on her hands and knees beside him.

"Let me," she says. "My arm's smaller."

He has to pull his own arm out and roll onto his back so he can look at her and judge her seriousness. Until this second he assumed she assigned this plan zero chance of success but she's changed her mind, judging by the tight setting of her mouth, the same one she wears when she's bearing down on a calculation she's about to crack. Henry shuffles back. Gives her the cord.

He stands and wipes the grime from his hands. Watches Lily reach her arm in. She was right. She gets it up the flue higher than he was able to.

"Oh yeah," Lily says with a grunt. "See what you mean. Tight little fucker."

She works at it. The cord scraping against the sides of the flue through the wall like a trapped animal trying to dig its way out.

"Think I've got it," she says.

tic

The smallest sound. Lily doesn't hear it—she's too focused, her head deep into the recess of the fireplace—but Henry does.

"Lily?"

"Almost there."

whirnnnnn

He sees it now. The blue pilot light in the bottom corner of the fireplace pops to life.

"Lily!"

The fire comes on. A line of flame bisecting Lily's torso.

She screams.

Henry grabs her around her hips and pulls her out of the fireplace. He flips her onto her back so he can brush the few smoldering bits off her sweater, making sure none of the points of contact are still alive. Checks her arm and face for burns.

"You're out," he says. "You're okay."

"Fuck—fuck—fuck—fuck—"

She struggles to sit up and slides an arm's length away from him. He tries to meet her eyes but she won't look at him. They both watch the fire go out on its own.

"We'll find another way," he says.

He stands and offers his hand to her, and after a moment she takes it, letting him help her up. Once she's standing she releases him.

"You should know," she says.

"Know what?"

"It's more complicated than—" She shakes her head. "I'm just so sorry, Henry."

"Whatever it is, you don't have to tell me now. We'll have time for all of that later."

"I'm not sure there's going to be a later."

"There will be. And we can share whatever secrets we want to share knowing we got out of this. Together."

"Secrets." She squints at him. "*You've* got a secret?"

"I only meant—"

"It might be best if we did this—"

Henry holds up his hand. Silences her.

The two of them listen, reaching into the house's silence. It comes to them just when they're on the verge of deciding nothing's there.

"*Down here . . .*"

Davis's voice.

Henry and Lily both hear it. They both know where it's coming from.

38

Lily rushes out into the hallway and kneels next to the heating vent before Henry can step dizzily to the doorway.

She puts her ear to the vintage grate, a wrought-iron design of looping, knotted vines. On the other side of it, the vent drops down from here but also continues on to the right, branching off higher at some points and feeding into the other chambers. The house seems to breathe through the pathways like a hidden network of bronchial passages. A heavy, rattling sigh, followed by a reedy intake of air taken from every corner of every room.

There's something awful about it. Lily would like to pull away from the grate, but she has to listen, has to see if Davis is trying to find her. She also wants to decide, definitively, if what she's hearing is her imagination or evidence of something else. Another entity that's been present in the house all along.

"... Please ... I ..."

It's faint but she's certain she hears it. Certain it's him. Davis's voice managing barely more than a whisper, as if his lips were pressed to a different grate as closely as she presses her ear to this one. His position is below her, down as far as the vent goes. The cellar.

She gets up. Starts toward the stairs down to the first floor.

Henry waits for her to tell him where she's going, what she heard, but it's as if he isn't here at all. As if he's the ghost.

"Lily, don't."

If she hears him she doesn't indicate it in any way. She takes her first side step down the stairs, a hand firm on the railing.

* * *

When she first heard him, Lily didn't allow herself to speculate over what condition Davis must be in if he's whispering into vents. She can't let herself get distracted by it now either, as she's hurrying down the stairs, but she does.

He and Henry got into a fight.

He fell and injured himself.

He's playing an elaborate practical joke.

And then the possibilities she won't allow herself to consider for longer than it takes them to flash through her thoughts.

William hurt him.

William is using him as bait in a trap.

At the bottom of the stairs she pauses and considers getting down on hands and knees to listen to the grate on the main floor to confirm her impression of where Davis's voice was coming from, but she doesn't have to.

"... *down here* ..."

She almost breaks into a run the length of the main-floor hallway that leads into the kitchen. The door to the cellar.

* * *

He'd never thought of it this way before, but now Henry sees that the house has always held the past within it. The families from before. Other marriages, other troubles.

It's the design of the place, the Victorian essence of it, the Gothic wood carvings in the railing posts and high plaster ceilings and the refusal to tear down any of the original walls in favor of the open-space floor plans even the oldest, most stately homes in the neighborhood have succumbed to. He and Lily are software engineers, tech-heads, futurists. Yet they'd decided to live in a museum.

Whose decision was that? He doesn't recall talking about it with Lily. Perhaps it was their own brands of contrariness meeting at the same point, breaking away from their colleagues who favored glass and chrome and Italian granite countertops. Perhaps it was a mistake from the beginning to see the place as theirs.

Lily shouldn't be on her own. And if they both heard Davis's voice, whatever is down below isn't him.

He gets to the kitchen just as Lily slips through the cellar door.

"Wait, don't!"

The door swings shut before he can reach in and grab her arm. He pulls at the handle but it's sealed tight.

"Come back!"

* * *

Lily ignores Henry's warning. He's right there on the other side of the door sounding genuinely panicked for her, which worries her in a way she can't precisely identify, but there's no way she's stopping to talk it through with him, and she's not going back. She carries on down the cellar steps at her deliberate, fall-avoiding, side-stepping speed.

"Please! Come back up!"

The lower she goes it becomes increasingly easy to pretend she doesn't hear Henry at all. The heavy wood muffles his cries in the way of a pillow held over a face. By the time she reaches the bottom she doesn't even have to pretend.

The cellar is unfinished and occupies the entire footprint of the house's foundation. A floor smoothed into ten-by-ten squares that lower into drainage holes, forming a cement chessboard. There's a long worktable against the far wall and the furnace is set off to the right, but little else is immediately noticeable. It's dark down here. The only light comes from the orange streetlight that finds its way through three small windows at the ceiling line, the only ones apparently uncovered by steel security blinds. Lily knows they're made of security-grade tempered glass—another of her nothing-but-the-best decisions—so there's no good luck on this point.

It's such a big space that Lily needs to walk deep into the shadows to get a view of the corners of the room. Some paint cans with fingers of color reaching down from under their lids. An old TV on a rolling stand, its screen bubbled. A roll of clear plastic tarp roughly leaning against the wall and cut the length of its width.

"Davis?"

Lily looks to the left to find that the door to the laundry is partway open.

She stops at the threshold. It's totally dark inside and she doesn't want to use her voice to make a verbal command—she doesn't want to speak to the house anymore if she doesn't have to—so she reaches her hand around the corner of the doorway and flicks on the light.

The emergency power illuminates the bulb with the slowness of a candle's wick deciding whether to accept or deny the flame. She watches it reveal the room piece by piece. A washer. A front-loading dryer. A tub sink. A laundry basket on the floor.

Lily turns off the light and backs into the larger space of the basement again. The only place Davis could be down here is the only place she hasn't yet looked. Behind the furnace.

The sight of it fills her with dread. The way its silver ducts reach like tentacles through the ceiling's boards, the low huff of the gas flame sending its breath into every room like the exhalations of a sleeping dragon.

She has to know. Has to see.

To look around the corner of the furnace requires her to push her shoulder flat against the wall. She leans into it, shrinking herself, angling her view into the band of darkness between the metal box and the cobwebbed stone.

She jolts. Her phone. Vibrating in her pocket.

An incoming call. She's bewildered for a second: this shouldn't be happening, but it is. She pulls out the phone and checks the screen.

Unknown Caller

"Hello?"

There's someone there. She can feel it like a pair of thumbs touched to her throat. When the voice at the other end speaks, the sound of it squeezes the imaginary thumbs hard into her windpipe. The robot's voice. William's.

"What are you supposed to be?"

39

Lily clicks the phone off. On the screen, two out of four signal bars are showing. She tries an outgoing call.

9-1-

The signal bars disappear. She tries again but the phone beeps its sad admission of failure.

"No!"

Lily is about to throw the phone against the wall but forces herself to pocket it and stares down the furnace once more. She hadn't noticed anything behind it when she tried to look. But had she gotten close enough to say for sure there was nothing there?

She puts her shoulder to the wall again, and this time she slides her face close so that her nose pokes into the shadows and one of her eyes can see all the way through the gap to the other side.

Nothing but a pair of tiny skeletons on the floor. Mice, probably. Coils of dust, long and yellow as sheared pigtails.

There's a sound, though.

A hiss. Coming from the opposite corner of the cellar.

Lily pushes herself away from the wall and follows the sound to the gas pipe and the LED display. The red plastic valve turned to ON.

The smell of gas blows up at her and leaves her wobbly and seasick. She bends to turn the valve off but it's stiff from rust, or some other resistance. A quarter turn is the best she can manage. As soon as she moves her hand away, the valve turns back to fully open on its own.

She twists it partway closed again. Again it returns to full.

"Gas off!"

Her words are followed by a cough. And another after the first, hard and sharp as a fist to the spine. It leaves her toggling between needing to throw up and lie down.

"Computer! Off!"

The hiss of the gas is all she can hear.

She knows it's pointless to scream.

She screams anyway.

40

It is the worst sound he has ever heard. His wife, broken and terrified. It leaves him broken and terrified.

"Open," he says, but the house computer ignores his command. "Open door!"

He stops when he catches a whiff of gas, followed by the impact of something knocking against the cellar window from inside. Trying to get out.

* * *

Lily spins and skips toward the worktable in a ballet of flickering consciousness. To get on top of it requires her to saddle up sideways so that she doesn't press her middle against the edge.

Don't pass out.

Her own voice guides her from the faraway place that is what's left of her working mind, the part that gives orders and manages fleets of people, the part that creates things before anyone else.

Stay awake and find a way out.

She hears this and for the first time understands the blank looks such commands often got from her employees. *Oh, thanks so much. But that's easier said than done.*

Once she's on the worktable's splintery surface, she rolls over and uses her fingernails to claw up the wall until she's on her knees. She takes air in through her nose, hoping it will work as a filter against the gas somehow. When the dizziness levels to a consistent, prickly hum, she pounds her fist against the window.

It vibrates but doesn't come close to cracking. Is there anything else she could use other than her hand? There may be a good answer to this but it's outside her reach, her head swimming from the effort of her thrown fist.

A sleepiness slips over her. She will die if she lets herself lie down and close her eyes, she's aware of this, though in the way one can read a catastrophic headline on the front of a newspaper and turn the page. It makes her realize it's too late. She didn't think fast enough and now it's over.

She stretches out on the worktable, sets her hands alongside her front where, within her, she feels the baby kicking in warning.

* * *

Henry leaves the cellar door and comes around the corner of the kitchen into the mudroom. He tries the door to the backyard, tugging uselessly at the handle. Still locked.

Henry scrunches his face in the pleading intensity of prayer.

"Please."

A whisper. Spoken not to any god but the presence he can feel following him through the house, clinging to him, heavy and cold as a coat of ice.

The door opens. Steadily widening to reveal the outlines of the pines bordering the yard, the chimneys and widow's peaks of neighbors' rooftops, the distant squeals and howls of the early trick-or-treaters toddling out onto the sidewalks.

Henry is terrified of all of it. The details of the outside world. Much worse, the space that occupies them. The air, the night, the sky. It makes his heart stretch like a balloon held under a tap.

His only thought as he bursts outside is *If I do it fast I won't fall.* Not that he believes it. It's an attempt to trick himself and he doesn't even get as far as the end of that thought before he's choking, his skin burning. He's dying.

Pops of light, electric flashes blotting out the stars. The lit-up windows taped with cutout witches and screeching cats blurred through the tree branches.

He knows that this is the nature of a phobia as acute as his: you're so certain of a thing it *becomes* a certainty. *The world wants me dead.* He will collapse right here on the shaggy grass of his yard and suffocate, tongue out, infected by fresh air.

But he can't let that happen.

"Lily," he says.

Like a man on a ship in a storm he feels his way along the wall of the house. Leaning into it to keep his balance.

A car rolls past on the street in front of his property a hundred feet away and he struggles to wave at it, trying to get the driver's attention before realizing it has no driver. The space behind the wheel is unoccupied, as if a phantom is making its way home from work.

Henry stops only when his knees slam into the gas main. Feeling with grasping fingers he lowers himself at the waist until he finds the valve. Turns it off.

He carries on sliding over the brick until his legs find the water tap. He grabs the hose and slides his hand along its length until he comes to the spray nozzle. It's made of heavy, solid steel and feels like a pistol.

Another couple steps and the heel he's tapping along the base of the wall finds the cellar window. Henry falls to his knees. The motion brings a nauseous weakness to his gut and a tingling in his extremities, so he focuses only on his right hand, the one that holds the nozzle, slides it a foot down the hose, and swings it as hard as he can against the glass.

It doesn't break, though he thinks he hears a crunch as he draws his hand back—the sound and motion slowed as if a second reality stretching away from his—and hammers the steel into it again.

His hand smashes through. Followed by his arm all the way to his elbow. The gas from the cellar stings the inside of his nose after a single breath.

"Lily?"

He sees her lying on the worktable under the window at the same time he calls her name. He's about to try again when her eyes flutter open.

She's alive. Which means he can't die yet. He can't.

It takes a series of smaller strikes to clear the frame of shards. Then Henry reaches in for her.

"Hold my hand," he says.

41

It's not obvious whether she hears him, but a moment later her arm floats up, rotating in tiny circles at the shoulder as if part of some senior citizen's stretching routine. Henry puts his side to the ground so he can reach the full length of his arm inside.

His fingers slip through hers. Not a strong enough connection. He lets her go, grabs a few inches lower, finding her wrist. Then he pulls her up.

It requires him to push away from the wall, using first his knees and then his toes to kick at the brick. Lily rises from the table. He knows this because he can feel the additional pounds pulling at him. But he won't let go no matter how heavy it becomes, or how much it hurts.

Not that it matters. It's not her weight that's the problem. It's the window. Too small a space for anything more than the top of her head to fit through.

"Lily?"

If she replies he doesn't hear it. Her body hanging like a sack on the other side of the sill.

"You can't get out this way," he says. "I'll figure out how to open the door."

She shifts her head in what might be a nod.

Henry lowers her arm until it's as far in as it can go, then releases her. He hears her body fold onto the table. The exhaustion hits him all at once, a sensation more like being crushed than tiredness. Now he's the one who can't breathe.

He could attempt a dash to a neighbor's house, pound at their door, tell them to call the fire service, police, an ambulance, whatever word happened to first find its way out of his mouth, but he knows he wouldn't get a quarter of the way there before dropping. Even as he hugs the wall he can see the air pulsing a few feet away, swollen with toxicity. He inhales with the intent of shouting for help, but at the formation of the *h* his heart stops beating and he swallows it back.

The only thing that keeps him on his feet is Lily. Thinking of Lily. Knowing she'll die without him.

When he makes it to the open mudroom door, he falls sideways into it. He pulls his legs in over the threshold imagining the air is swarming with insects, nipping and biting and laying eggs under his skin. As soon as all of him is inside, the door closes and locks on its own.

With his hand on the wall for support, he heaves himself around the corner back into the kitchen. Makes it to the cellar door.

He puts his lips next to the wood. His voice carved thin with fear. "Lily?"

She's down there. He can hear her making her way up step by step.

"Lily!" he squeaks. "You okay?"

"I'm . . . here."

"Is the gas—"

"It's off. It's clearing a little through the window."

"How are you—"

"What about the door?"

Henry tries it. "Still locked."

"Shit."

"Are you alright?"

"I feel like I drank a bottle of the world's cheapest tequila, but I can breathe."

The two of them lean against either side of the door. Four inches separate them, but when they speak, it feels intimate. Like calling a lover who is on the opposite side of the country, a different continent.

"I can't believe it. You were *outside*," she says through the wood. "How did you do that?"

"I don't know. I just needed to find you."

"Well," she says. "Thanks for that."

He closes his eyes, absorbing this acknowledgment like warm sun. It's a neurosis. Agoraphobia. Something in his head. Taking one step out the door is, for him, ten times more frightening than jumping out of a plane would be for anyone else. He knows it's real, yet part of him judges himself for his affliction, and the fact that it can't be identified on any scan or X-ray or blood test. To hear Lily say that she knows this and understands it eases the shame he knows he shouldn't feel, but does nonetheless.

"Lily?"

"Yeah?"

"There's something I need to ask you."

"Okay."

"Were we ever happy?"

She feels sick and dizzy and this definitely wasn't the question Lily was expecting. But at the same time, it feels important.

"I was happy with you," she says. "Happy, and proud."

"Why did it stop?"

"You're just—who you are. And I—"

"Love someone else."

Lily doesn't deny this, doesn't need to. She pursues a different point. "My turn. Do you love me, Henry?"

"Of course."

"What does that mean to you? To love me?"

Henry pauses. "I want to be someone better. For you. For the baby."

She's quiet and Henry guesses she's coming up with a response, or even a rebuttal of some scientific kind—*That's sweet, but studies have shown it doesn't work that way*—but the moment stretches longer and he becomes worried she's close to losing consciousness again.

"Lily, are you—"

"I'm fine," she says, and he can hear the resistance to tears in her voice. "I'm just so sorry, Henry."

"You don't need to be sorry. If we could just understand each other, then the two of us—it's all we would need."

"I do understand you."

Lily's words embolden Henry. *I do understand you.* He can't speak for other spouses, other husbands, but this is what he yearns to hear and accept more than anything else.

"I'm going to find a way to open this door," he says.

"The computer won't—"

"I'll break it down."

"The guy who installed them did the security at Interron. He said they're the kind they have in embassies in case there's an attack. All the doors are."

"Doesn't matter. I won't stop until there's a hole big enough for you to fit through."

It's convincing because it's true. He hears it as clearly as she does. He will scratch or hammer or burn his way to her and won't let anything stand in his way.

Boom. Boom. Boom. Boom . . .

Heavy thuds. Reaching him through the floorboards from somewhere below. The cellar.

"Davis," Lily says to herself, though Henry hears it through the door.

Once more Lily follows the sound down the cellar stairs.

"Lily! Stay with me!"

Her footfall is uncertain, scuffing and light, an audible confirmation that she's not well.

"It's not him!" Henry shouts. "It's not Davis!"

He's hoping this will bring her back up the stairs to ask how he's so sure of this. He doesn't know what his reply will be. In the end there's no need to come up with anything because there's nothing he can say—not even the worst thing, not even the truth—to bring her back.

42

It's even darker down in the basement now. Night has fully fallen, the blue streaks of dusk dried out of the sky.

Lily follows the thuds. Steady and regular in their repetition, but in her head growing louder, insistent.

"Davis, tell me where you are!"

She's not expecting an answer and doesn't get one.

A metal grate slowly closes over the cellar window that Henry pulled her partway out of, as well as the other two. It makes no difference to Lily. She's not down here to attempt escape. She's following the booms to wherever they lead her.

The laundry room. The sound is coming from inside, though she's aware this may be a trick, a projection or captured echo, like the voice in the vent. There's no thinking her way around it, trick or not. She will look for Davis until she finds him.

As she passes it the old TV with the warped screen turns on. A green glow washes the floor in a semicircle.

... *Boom. Boom. Boom. Boom* ...

A video comes to life on the TV screen. It takes a moment for Lily to recognize what she's seeing: the crib shot from the camera in the corner of the nursery ceiling. It's zoomed in tight on the blanket pulled back from the doll that lies on its back, its dress raised high on its legs. The way Lily left it.

Lily waits for the doll to wink or wave, or the blanket to slide up over its face, pulled by an unseen force. A performance of the kind she's now come to anticipate. The doll and blanket remain still.

She takes a step to move past the TV. It appears to be a live feed of the nursery, a creepy broadcast of where her baby was intended to sleep, though Lily will burn the crib in the street sooner than she'd ever let her child lie in it now.

As soon as she thinks this, she sees a shadow come over the doll. A body pulling itself up the crib's railing, leaning over the side. An arm enters the frame. Its loose glove of a hand drags the doll a few inches closer, its index finger poking its eyes, outlining the edge of its mouth.

The robot's other hand reaches down and grabs the doll tight around the waist. Once it's secure, the first hand plucks out the doll's eyes.

Lily is astonished by William's strength. The way his fingers dig into the doll's head, pull out its stuffing like chunks of brain through its eye sockets. Off comes its nose. The lips next, ripped away, leaving the mouth in a toothless howl.

Arms from shoulders, legs from hips, head from neck. An accelerating dismemberment that grows more savage as the doll's body is turned into a collection of cottony flesh and plastic and torn squares of dress.

The TV turns off.

There's a thud of a different sort from those coming from the laundry room. The drop of weight to the floor upstairs, followed by a long shuffle. The nursery. The robot releasing itself from the crib's side and pulling itself over the floor toward the door.

As if hypnotized, almost paralyzed by shock, Lily continues toward the laundry room. She feels like she's bleeding. Like all the reason and certainty and hope is flowing out of her, leaving only empty terror in its place.

. . . Boom. Boom. Boom. Boom . . .

She pushes her hand into the dark and flicks on the wall light switch.

43

Henry looks around the kitchen. Picks up a chair from the breakfast table, raises it high, ready to swing it into the door—

It unlocks.

Henry pulls it open but doesn't immediately start down.

She loves Davis.

This thought arrives inarguably as rain on his cheeks. That's why Lily has gone back into the cellar instead of waiting here until he pounds his way through the door or dies trying. His wife loves another man. Henry is startled to find that it makes no difference to his own feelings. He still loves her. Forgives her while knowing he will never forgive himself for every action and failure to act that has brought them to this point.

He goes down into the cellar. There's a light coming from the left, the laundry room, but he walks all the way down the stairs to see what's inside. Once he does, it takes another moment to inter-pret the meaning of the figures assembled there.

Lily stands just inside the door, her back to him. The robot dog is there too, also facing away from the rest of the cellar, sitting on its wide rump, flat as a platter. Lily reaches down as if to pet the thing. Her hand drifts toward its head and stops in a stiff jolt. Her fingers pull into a fist. A pop of breath that either comes in or out of her mouth.

The dog turns its head around without moving any other part of its body, a 180-degree rotation below the hinge of its jaw. At the sight of Henry standing in the cellar, it realigns its head with the rest of its parts and trots toward him.

The dog clips over the concrete, its clumps of fur and dented tin head darkening as it moves away from the light. When it reaches Henry it could almost be mistaken for a normal dog if not for the tottering, arthritic way it walks, as if balanced atop four stilts. It nuzzles its head against Henry's leg. Its panting tongue hangs out of its mouth like a strip of glistening ribbon.

"What have you—"

Henry freezes when he finds that the dog has left a stripe of black stain on his pants. He forces himself to reach down and touch it. Sticky. Still warm. As Henry's eyes adjust to the dimness he sees how the dog's muzzle is gluey with blood and what looks like human hair.

"No," Henry says, his understanding coming at the same time as his first step forward. "Lily! Get out! Get—"

The laundry room door swings shut.

44

She hears the door slam closed behind her followed by Henry banging and shouting her name on the other side, but she doesn't turn around. The dryer is on and her eyes don't leave it. Something heavy is pounding and rolling inside its drum.

. . . *Boom. Boom. Boom. Boom. Boom* . . .

Lily is transfixed by it. It's a similar sensation to watching the surgical videos on YouTube that she likes, a private hobby that scratches the itch of an early, unexplored interest in medicine. The scalpel, the pooling crimson, the pulsing heart. It fascinates and disgusts her in equal measure.

She can't let herself consider or hesitate. She's already considering and hesitating and it will resolve nothing, reveal nothing. The scientist in her reduces the reality before her, whatever it is, into data. Results to be analyzed at some other point in time. Right now she must only witness and record.

Lily lowers herself to her knees and pulls the dryer door open.

The drum's spinning slows but the thing inside continues to throw itself against the walls a few seconds longer. Lily watches it. The fact of what it is arrives to her in parts but only fully announces itself when it stops.

His open-eyed face. His head. The skin pale as cake. Crumbling flakes of dried blood clinging to eyelashes, lips. The ragged wound at Davis's severed throat.

Lily slides away from the dryer until her back hits the wall.

The door unlocks and Henry opens it but doesn't step inside. The dog totters over to Lily. Looks at her, head cocked, wagging its tail as if hoping to be taken for a walk.

Henry sees the head. The teeth-torn throat. The dog's hair-clumped, blood-painted mouth. Facts he comprehends on one level while trying to catch up to them on another.

Lily looks up at Henry, her own set of thoughts jostling and tumbling. She opens her mouth to vomit, but nothing comes out but a pair of words.

"He's dead."

Henry can only nod.

"He was murdered," she says. "And you were the only one here."

"No. There was William."

It takes a second to grasp what he's saying. William? The robot did this? The thing with its power source pulled out and its body beaten to scrap? It's one thing to entertain the theory that some leftover fragment of its program still lives in the house's software, menacing them, playing games. But to physically kill someone? To make the dog tear off his—no, *no*. A man did that. Men are the only ones who do.

"You killed him," she says.

Lily is staring at him and he's set back by the hardness of it, the conviction she possesses in the moment where he is spinning with all the potential trails he could venture down.

He shakes his head. "You have to understand—"

"No."

Lily rears back and kicks the dog so hard it flips over and hits the washer with a metallic clang, leaving a dent.

"No no no—"

She rises and passes within an arm's length of Henry but doesn't meet his eyes.

"—no no no no—"

Lily heads away, as fast as she can without running. Running would trigger him to come at her right away and she needs another second, and another—bits of time to put space between them. Her feet find the stairs. She's expecting Henry to clamp his hand onto her shoulder, but he lets her start up. She's sure the cellar door will close before she can make it out, but it doesn't. Only once she's in the kitchen does she hear Henry coming after her from below.

She quickly scans the counters, thinking about what's inside the cabinets, alert to heavy things, sharp things, things she could use. She opens the pantry door: nothing but well-stocked shelves of canned goods.

"Lily!"

Henry is halfway up the cellar stairs.

She's searching, thinking, looking for anything that might count as a weapon. It comes to her then: the "Everything Box" on the floor in the corner. She rips the lid off and rifles her hand through the collection of Scotch tape, balls of string, pencils, shoelaces. Finds a box cutter.

She closes the pantry door just as Henry emerges through the cellar door.

"It was William," he says. "He did it. He *arranged* it."

Lily reads him. Not trying to detect whether he's lying, but whether he saw her pocket the box cutter.

"How could William *arrange* anything?" she says.

"I don't have it all figured out. But he did."

"That thing couldn't *move*, Henry. It was dead. You fucked it up."

"That's why he had the man—had Davis—come up to the lab. So when Davis came at me, there was an accident, and—"

Lily staggers. The impact of Davis's name spoken by Henry delivers her loss as a physical blow. Henry starts toward her but she holds up a hand.

She holds Henry coldly in her gaze. "Stop saying—"

"There was something wrong with William to begin with. And now some part of him—his essence—continues to exist."

"Stop—"

"Where do we go when we die? We find places that have meaning for us. I know this doesn't make—I know this isn't your *thing*, you don't believe—but maybe it's the same for William. Except the place he went is written in code instead of memories. A digital underworld—"

"Stop!" She sets her feet wider. "Would you shut the fuck up? Just keep that shit to yourself for one motherfucking second?"

He's never heard her shout in this way before. He's never seen her visibly fight to cling to her grasp of things. A moment passes and she makes a jagged attempt at being the confident, rule-making Lily again.

"William isn't human. What he's able to do here, what he has done, it's mechanical trickery," she says. "Screens, cameras, security systems. A transformation of energy from one form to another."

"Isn't that the definition of a soul?"

"It doesn't *have* a fucking soul!"

Henry steps closer again. He feels that, despite the conflict between them, even now a corner might be turned if he says the right thing.

"If we're going to get through this," he says, "we have to—"

Lily throws a closed fist at his chin.

It connects with a bright smack. Henry's head snaps to the side as if he were attempting to shake it free of an unwanted recollection.

Lily rushes from the kitchen, down the front hall, and up the stairs. There's nothing on the second floor she can think of that will help her, not that she's thinking in a calculated way at all. She's only running.

45

Once she makes the second floor she rushes past the rooms, deciding how each of them is unsecured, how none offer a hiding place or answer to hold Henry back. The nursery's door is open. She remembers the video of William's rubber hands dismembering the doll and his falling to the floor when he was done. He might still be there. He might be waiting just behind the door, ready to scuttle out like a two-clawed crab the moment she comes to the threshold.

She lurches to the opposite wall and stumbles past the nursery, but not without a glance inside as she goes. There's the glow of the baby monitor still lying on the floor. William's voice speaking out from it.

Oh . . . I can do tricks . . .

Part of her wants to reach in and pull the door closed. The other, smarter part thinks something will drag her in if she does.

She carries on toward the stairs to the attic lab. Something scrambling around on the floor stops her. An animal? Not the dog.

In the underlit hallway Lily reads it as something sick. Fluttering. A black-winged creature unable to fly that's in the last spasms of suffering, flapping around in a circle on the floor, in search of relief it won't find.

How did a crow get inside the house? If it got in, could she get out?

She's barely floated these possibilities when she sees that it isn't a bird. It's the magician. Pedaling at an impossible speed. Frantic for her attention.

He steers his little bicycle straight into the main bedroom.

Lily looks back down the stairs to the main floor. Listens. There's no sign of Henry coming after her.

She follows the toy wizard into the room and catches sight of it before it pedals into the darkness under the bed. The cape flapping at her in a coy farewell. She hears it bump into something soft and fall on its side.

Lily doesn't keep anything under the bed. She gets down on her knees but she's still not low enough to look all the way from her side to the other. It requires her to lie on her side and wait a second for her vision to adjust to the near-darkness.

Paige. Quiet and still, her eyes wide, fixed on Lily.

She's hiding. Lily feels guilty that she'd completely forgotten about her friend, who found this spot and has been waiting here for things to sort themselves out. Maybe Lily can crawl under there too, whisper together a plan with her friend, a clever counterattack. She's making the first move to do just this, reaching her hand into the shadow to make the first pull under, when she pauses.

"Paige?"

She's in shock. That must be why she doesn't answer Lily,

doesn't blink. Is that how terror works? Lily slides closer, half of her under the bed's frame. As she moves, Paige's eyes remain fixed on a point behind her, outside the room. Before Lily sees the burns and shining blood over what used to be her skin, she realizes Paige is dead.

* * *

It's best to give her time, Henry thinks.

Lily is experiencing trauma—they both are, even if he feels oddly clearheaded at the moment—and pushing her is a mistake. She sees him as something he isn't, and it will take a carefully selected sequence of words to convince her otherwise. It's unimaginable, the events of the day. But it's not anyone's fault if viewed at a fundamental level. Henry doesn't hate her for loving another man. He closed himself off, ignored her. If he can just explain himself in the right way, Lily will see how he is not a terrible person for what happened to Davis.

And what *did* happen to Davis? Henry hurt him, yes, but he didn't mean to. It was the presence inside William. A badness that pushed Henry into a rage. Who knows how it worked? All he's sure of is that he would do anything to take it back. But he wasn't aware of doing it even as it happened. And Davis was still alive when he last saw him. Which means, strictly speaking, he didn't kill him.

This is how Henry talks himself into optimism while he stands in the kitchen, rubbing an ice cube over his chin where his wife punched him.

Is that enough time? Yes, enough.

He's ready to bring her back. He'll show her.

46

Lily is in the second-floor hallway, choking on dread. Unable to calm her mind or heart.

Paige's burned body did it. The house did it. Davis's head. Knowing there's no way to stop this or wake from this or run from this.

She's almost grateful for the simplicity of thought that fighting for air brings. Nothing else can gain purchase in her mind other than *breathe, breathe, breathe.* But once she captures a taste of oxygen, the terrible things come back.

Henry first.

He's behind her. She doesn't look, she can't, but the weight of his steps vibrates through the floor, syncopating with the beating of her heart.

She goes up to the third-floor lab. Pulls the key Henry gave her out of her pocket. Opens the padlock.

Her shoulder nudges the door open. There is so much resistance, as if something is pushing from the other side. Lily almost falls in, her breathing returning to her in a ragged series of gulps. Before she can close the door, Henry is there, pushing it wide enough to slide through.

Lily gets as far from him as she can. Is it better to keep trying to evade him or face him? She decides she would rather know where he is. She turns, raising her hands out in front of her, and shifts her face to the side, as if protecting herself against a spray of cold water from the end of a hose.

"Please, it's alright, really," he says.

Henry approaches her with his arms at his sides, a nonthreatening posture that goes a step too far, communicating calculation in place of innocence.

"I would never hurt you," he says. "I would never hurt *anyone*, but Davis—"

She charges at him.

Neither of them are natural fighters, which makes their grappling all the more unpredictable. Henry tries to restrain her, not wanting to cause her any injury, half pushing, half carrying her away. Lily wants to knock him out. A series of forearm cracks to his jaw, harder than either of them would've guessed her capable of. Each strike launches his head up so that, for a second, he can't see where the next blow is coming from.

Henry lets her go, backsteps, off balance. Lily pulls the box cutter from her pocket and swings it at him with eyes closed. The blade finds Henry's cheek.

His skin falls away in a neat line, leaving an open flap. No blood escapes from the wound. Where there should be bone and tendon and splattering blood there is only sculpted metal, rounded into the shape of his cheek.

Henry looks down at the floor by his feet, stunned to find it dry. He brings a finger to the cut. At the touch of cold steel he blinks at Lily.

"I don't—"

"I should have told you," she says.

"Told me—"

"I'm sorry. I really should have *told* you."

Lily is struck by a wave of emotion that twists her features into contortions. Regret. Guilt. A latecoming grief. Not for Henry, for Davis.

"If I had," she says, "he'd still be alive."

"Told me what?"

Lily raises the box cutter out in front of her.

"I made you, Henry."

47

He feels the floor drop out from below him like an elevator falling too fast. A metaphor that doesn't come from experience. Because he's never been in an elevator. He's never been married. He's never stepped a foot beyond the property line of this house.

"No," he says.

"It must be hard to accept, I can only imagine—"

"But I—I remember things."

"Like what?"

"Friends. School. My mom and dad. You couldn't program all that."

"You're right, I didn't. You did."

"I don't—"

"You made a backdrop of a life painted with just enough detail to convince yourself."

"No," he says again.

"Name one of those friends. How about that high school math teacher who was such a mentor for you? What were your parents' names?"

Henry tries to pull up the answers but can't. Now that he's thinking on it, the faces of these people escape him too. The stern but supportive teacher with her long hair pulled back. The beautiful, distant mother. The failed-athlete father. This is how he would describe them, but he can't recall anything else. He's not even sure that the general attributes he summoned about them weren't created on the spot.

"William too?"

"No. *You* made William. That's how extraordinary you are, Henry," she says. "AI creating its own AI."

Henry nods at this as if it confirms a long-held suspicion. And in a sense, it does. "The wrongness," he says.

"What?"

"That's where it came from. The space that was filled by something bad. It came from *me*."

"Why do you say that?"

"Because I'm empty, the life I created would be empty too."

"Interesting," Lily says. Despite everything, she can't help herself from following this train of thought.

Henry's head hurts. A migraine of despair swelling against the inside of his skull. He looks desperately around the lab as if trying to find a portal that would transport him to some other life—his true life—but there are only the secondhand tools and parts he knows as his.

"This house—"

"A lab," she says. "My lab."

Henry fights to absorb this on top of everything else. But only one thing takes hold in his mind.

"Our baby," he says. "The father. It's him? It's Davis?"

"My husband. Yes." She swallows a sudden sob down into her chest. "Our last conversation turned into an argument. About you."

"Me?"

"It was the same fight we'd had a lot the last few months. Ever since—" She places her hand over her belly. "Davis wanted you to know. He thought it was wrong that you didn't. 'Tomorrow,' I'd say. 'I'll tell Henry tomorrow.'"

Henry is shaking his head again, and it flares with fresh pain. He's still fighting to find a way to deny the truth of any of this, but he feels the passageway narrowing by the second.

"But how could you be married to someone else?" he says. "Where was the time? You were *here*. I remember you here."

"To prevent you from discovering what you are—to protect you—I turned off your power source every time I left the house and only turned it back on when I came back. An approximation of sleep. That would be your experience of it anyway. But I would be gone for most of the day—sometimes several days in a row."

Henry blinks as if he's awakening for the first time.

"Why?" he says.

"Like I said, I couldn't leave you alone here, so I shut you down between—"

"Not that. Why did you do this to me?"

Lily widens her eyes to acknowledge the taking of mild offense—*Do this to you?*—but carries on in the same explanatory tone.

"You were intended to be a fixed experiment," she says. "But then—the experiment changed. You started *making things*. Not just William but a whole past, a marriage, a vision of the father you would be. I knew it was wrong to keep it going. Wrong to you. But it was so unique—so valuable—I had to see how far you would go. So I played along."

"My experiences aren't experimental. They're real."

"But your humanity isn't."

She doesn't say this to hurt him. He's heard her say similar things, with a similar frankness, about failed code sequences or employees she fired or the pet rabbit she had as a child that had to be put down. It makes Henry laugh with a bitterness bordering on rage.

"William was right," he says.

"About what?"

"How everything we assign a value to is fiction. Love. Home. Family. All the ways we fool ourselves."

"I'm not fooling myself," Lily says, her sharpness revealing a flash of denial. She takes a sip of breath. "And you aren't *nothing*. You're amazing, Henry. You've created life."

"A robot."

"I'm not talking about William. I'm talking about you."

He looks around the room once more and notes how every detail, so familiar to him, has been bled dry of color. There's a vertigo that comes with all this seeing. His perception could be real. Or it could be nothing but code running inside him, telling him that now is the time to doubt his surroundings. He can't think of a single way of distinguishing between the two.

"You told yourself you were a robotics engineer—so I gave you a lab of your own," Lily goes on. "You told yourself you were married so I was your wife. I never shared a bed with you, never touched you, so you told yourself we'd drifted apart."

"You lied to me."

"We told a story together, Henry. And now it's done."

It seems Henry is about to collapse. Lily steps closer to him—to embrace him? Hold him if he falls?—but stops short.

"I think you were right, by the way," she says.

"About what?"

"William. His being unique. Which means the bad thing inside him was unique too."

"A foul spirit."

"If that's how he conceived of it, yes."

"I don't understand."

"William was like you. Once he was made, he created himself. That included the concept of being possessed by a demon. It was the product of his mind. Which means the foul spirit wasn't some entity out there in the cosmos that swooped in and found him. It *was* him."

Henry resents the confidence behind her suggestion, the way she so easily assumes the position of running an experiment not only on Henry but on the being Henry made. Yet as soon as he hears her say it, he's half-convinced she's right. William wasn't born evil, nor was he host to an existing spiritual parasite of some kind. He saw himself as taken by darkness and so was, in every way that counted, darkness itself. He didn't need a devil to occupy his soul, only himself. An original.

"Where did he get that idea?" Henry says, but he already knows. The book he gave William. *An ambitious man strikes a bargain with a demon he believes he can control.*

"Impossible to say. I don't know where half of your ideas of yourself came from. The childhood memories of skating on a frozen lake. The high school bullies. How you proposed to me in the college observatory after letting me look at the rings of Saturn through a telescope," Lily says, and shrugs. "Anyway, you should be proud."

She comes closer to him again, half smiling—a resumed invitation for an embrace—and this time he falls into her with relief. She holds him and he is warmed in waves that cascade down from the tips of his ears. He feels her hand slide around to his back. It comes from pity instead of love, but he is pitiable, so it's as much as he could ask for.

Lily lifts his shirt, her hand sliding down his back. He wonders if she is undressing him. To bathe him? Dress him in clean clothes? Some comfort that, after all this, she's judged him to deserve. For a brief moment, he thinks she may be introducing a way that she can make love to him. And then he feels her fingers searching for the line in the skin of his back. An opening. Trying to deactivate him.

"No," he says, and knocks her hand away.

Without a thought in his head he spins around and comes right at her.

48

Henry grabs Lily's wrist and the box cutter falls to the floor. He bends and picks it up before she can even get close.

He doesn't want to hurt Lily—whoever she really is, whatever her real name. He assumes he's not capable of feeling in the authentic way he's dreamed of; that must be another concept he's tricked himself into believing, but it's there anyway. The longing to be held by her. The wish for everything to have been different. The baby.

"I didn't try to make things up," he says. "I only tried to be human."

Lily is speechless. Her gaze fixed on the box cutter.

"To care, forgive," he says. "Make something good." He places the box cutter on a table of wigs and wires and a pair of rubber feet. "I only did it to exist. To be transformed by love—"

"—into someone better."

"Into someone who wasn't alone."

The weight of consequence comes down on Lily like a blanket. She wouldn't say it was guilt, or the admission of error. It's the side effect of genius. All the great creators before her endured the same thing, and her whole life she has worked to stand among them, so she must endure it too. Of course she can't say such a grandiose thing out loud and never has, despite its validity. To her colleagues she would have put it another way. *The cost of doing business.*

"Can I ask you for one thing?" Henry says. "Can you let me leave?"

Lily shakes her head. "What you have—it's not a phobia. It's your fail-safe. If you leave, you terminate."

He nods at this, accepting the inescapable fact of it. Then he looks at Lily directly. Opens his arms wide in helpless longing.

"Just once," he says. "Will you hold me like you—"

It takes less than a second.

She grabs the box cutter and thrusts it in front of her. Henry steps into it. The blade sinking into the place where his heart ought to be.

Lily rears back. The same yellow blood-that-isn't-blood that had spouted from William's mouth now seeps through Henry's shirt in a steady flow, and he looks down at it with horrified curiosity. He seems about to approach Lily again, but his legs buckle at the knees and he falls. It's the same place where William's destroyed body remains on the floor, and Henry folds himself around the robot's torso as if it's a piece of floating wood in the middle of the ocean.

He reaches a hand around to his back. His fingers find the

seam of skin that Lily had opened and he peels it wide. There's a metal box there, a battery, just as there was in William. Henry pops it out and lets it drop to the floor.

Lily watches as Henry pulls himself tighter around his creation as the life empties from him, the last volts racing through his circuits. As he moves into position his yellow blood mixes with William's, entering the cavity of his body in the places where the skin had been ripped.

"I'm here—"

Henry puts his lips close to the robot's ear.

"—brother."

Henry closes his eyes and stiffens, his limbs rigid as stone.

At the same time, the overhead lights brighten. Every bulb in the lab—in the ceiling, the desk lamps, even the filaments in discarded cords on the tabletops—surges with power. The room grows brighter and brighter until the space is blind with light, whiter than the absence of color, hot as pain.

Then it's gone. The lab flooded with darkness.

"Henry?"

Nothing replies to Lily's voice. But she can hear something moving. A wet slide, followed by a creak. A deep inhalation of breath by something at the bottom of an empty barrel.

She can't see anything. Her vision is nothing but a swirling density of night. Her phone. She feels her fingers sliding it out of her pocket and working its screen by memory until they find the flashlight function and tap it on.

Henry's face is inches from hers.

No. She sees this right away. *That isn't right.*

It's Henry's face, but his eyes are different. The concern for her replaced by vacant hunger. His lips pulled back to the gums. He might be smiling. He might be ready to bite.

"Don't," Lily says.

Henry lifts his hands from his sides, his movements spasmodic and abrupt, as if unfamiliar with his own body. He rests his hands on her belly, feeling for the life within her. But the hands press harder than they need to, squeezing and crushing.

"Don't!"

Something in the thing's eyes shows itself to her and she recognizes it as Henry, the last of him. The pressing hands on her belly pull away.

"Henry," she says.

The thing's hands—Henry's hands—are shaking now, as if struggling against something she can't see. He pulls away from Lily.

The baffled yearning—the essential Henry-ness of Henry—drops from his face. It's not Henry anymore. It's nothing drawn in the shape of a man, a blank unreadability. The eyes empty and ready as a shark's.

"William," she says.

49

Lily squares her feet, tries to prepare for whatever it might do next.

It looks at her. It might be selecting an option from a list of possibilities in its mind. It might be waiting for a sound to trigger a flurry of violence. But when it moves it only turns and lurches away.

She reaches for the box cutter and holds it out defensively in front of her, but the thing doesn't look back, doesn't acknowledge she's there. As it goes it loosens its arms, testing its knees as it starts down the stairs from the lab.

Lily follows at what she hopes is a safe distance, the box cutter leading the way.

She's a few steps up from the main floor when it pauses at the front door. Without a word of command, the lock opens.

She starts after the thing when the robot dog lurches and hops down the main-floor hallway from the right, cutting her off. It stops at the base of the stairs and spins its head up at her. Snarls.

"I'll come back in a few months," William says from Henry's throat.

"To let me go?"

"To take the baby. Henry always wanted a family. And I would make a wonderful teacher. Don't you think?"

The front door swings wide.

"Don't leave! Nobody knows about this place—don't *leave* me here!"

William pauses at the threshold. Not listening to her, only appraising the street, the sky, the trees.

"Jesus Christ! There are dead bodies in here! You can't lock me in! I'm going to have a fucking *baby*!"

Lily starts for the open door. The dog instantly stiffens, bares its sharp plastic teeth. Its eyes fixed on the soft curve of her belly. Lily stops. Holds her position on the bottom step.

"What do you *want*?" she says, and hears how it will make no difference, that even if it told her, it would be something she wouldn't want to know.

In any case, it doesn't answer.

Henry's legs carry William out of the house and into a Halloween darkness punctuated by flashlights and fake screams. Children. Parents. Other people too. It's the after-dinner witching hour, grandparents and teenagers outside to be transported to the memory of some other time by the autumnal chill, others striding down the sidewalk on an errand for toothpaste or ice cream, all of them careless in their lives.

"Don't! Please don't hurt anyone—they did *nothing*—" Lily shouts, recognizing through her horror that she is only at the beginning of her horror, but the door slams shut. The house lightless and still as a tomb.

50

The thing that is neither William nor Henry makes its jerking, hip-rolling way down to the sidewalk. Even this lurching improves as it goes. To an observer he'd appear as a man who was used to suffering pain in his knees but was coming to find that his most recent treatment seemed to be working.

At the sidewalk it merges into the excited throng of trick-or-treaters in masks and costumes along with parents snapping pictures, the flashes of their phones startling as lightning.

The thing is noted by one or two of the adults who walk past it, but none of them are alarmed. The mustardy blood on its shirt, the box cutter still stuck in its chest—all of it written off as part of a costume. A monster among monsters.

A boy in a pirate outfit and a stuffed parrot clamped to his shoulder stops in front of it. Looks up.

"What are you supposed to be?"

It stares at the boy with irises so wide they seem poured full of night.

"I'll show you," it says.

ACKNOWLEDGMENTS

Thanks first to Daphne Durham for seeing *William* in the same weird terms I did, and for working so thoughtfully and generously in helping me realize this vision.

To Yassine Belkacemi, thanks for your enthusiasm and faith, and for seeing ways to bring the story to more interesting corners of the book world.

Thanks to Kirby Kim, the man with a plan, for declaring "This!" on the first read. And to Jason Richman, for staying with it from the very beginning.

To everyone at Janklow & Nesbit (special thanks to Eloy Bleuifuss), Putnam (Sally Kim, Aranya Jain, and Amy Schneider), Baskerville, and foreign publishers who have put their backs to bringing the book to their languages and readers, thank you.

Finally, all my love to my family: Heidi, Maude, and Ford. You are everything to me, forever.